What the critics are saying...

Winner of the National Reader's Choice Award

5 Hearts "These two stubborn individuals are very well-matched in energy, enthusiasm, sensuality, intelligence and wicked humor. The relationship evolving between them is so very hot and beautifully written by Ms. Barker..." ~ *The Romance Studio*

4 Stars "This is a romance that makes you believe the characters could really exist. The setting is described with the right amount of detail without drawing out every little detail. The characters are warm and just like people you may know. You won't want to put the book down until they realize they were meant to be together!" ~ *Romantic Times*

5 Cupids "**CHAMELEONS** is a superb read...The chemistry between Erica and Ryan is immediate and MS BARKER keeps it fevered and explosive throughout the story. I was especially impressed with the character's witty dialogue and how smart their relationship is...I cannot fully express how great this story is and how captivating Ryan and Erica are. As their many lesser secrets are revealed the larger ones become more ominous like a hibernating bear and when they come to light the way in which the characters handle them and their interchange is definitely worth the read. The many steamy moments between Erica and Ryan are also unforgettable and very hot...A great romantic and erotic read." ~ *Cupids Library Review*

Becky Barker

Chameleons

Cerridwen Press

A Cerridwen Press Publication

www.cerridwenpress.com

Chameleons

ISBN #1419955489

Edited by Ann Leveille
Cover art by Willo

Electronic book Publication December 2005
Trade paperback Publication September 2006

Cerridwen Press is an imprint of Ellora's Cave Publishing, Inc.®

Also by Becky Barker

A Matter of Trust

Hanchart Land

Prescott Pilots 1: Born to Fly

Prescott Pilots 2: Logan's Lady

Prescott Pilots 3: Loving Carly

About the Author

Becky Barker is a multi-published author whose steamy romance novels have been translated into more than a dozen foreign languages, into electronic format, and have been reissued in trade paperback as well as large print library editions.

Her personal hero is a former Marine who helped her create three pretty wonderful children. Rachel and her husband, Jerramy; Amanda and her husband, Jay; and Thad and his wife, Dara, all live within a few miles of Mom and Dad in rural Ohio.

Besides spending time with her family, Becky enjoys music, gardening, water sports and reading. She loves to hear from readers and can be reached through her website at BeckyBarker.com

Becky welcomes comments from readers. You can find her website and email address on her author bio page at www.cerridwenpress.com.

CHAMELEONS

Dedication

This one's for Buzz; my love, my heart and the wind beneath my wings.

Trademarks Acknowledgement

The author acknowledges the trademarked status and trademark owners of the following wordmarks mentioned in this work of fiction:

Stetson: John B. Stetson Company

Formica: The Formica Insulation Company

Styrofoam: Dow Chemical Company

Energizer: Eveready Battery Company

Boy Scouts of America: Boy Scouts of America Corporation

Jell-O: General Foods Corporation

Chapter One

Ryan Havens took a long swallow of beer and made a solemn pledge to himself. He'd never risk his heart again. Never. He was finished with love. Finished with emotions that left him edgy, uptight and aching. A man could live just fine without it, and that's what he intended to do from this night forward.

The chilled liquid slid down his throat, and he welcomed the stinging tartness. It was his fourth beer, one past his usual limit, but a man had a right to get shit-faced when the only women he'd ever loved gave birth to another man's baby.

His chest constricted at the thought. Katlyn. He wanted only the best for her, but damn, it still hurt.

Studying the now empty bottle and contemplating having another, he decided the hell with self-discipline and respectability. They were overrated anyhow, and he was bent on drowning his sorrows, just like the cowboys in those country songs who kept cryin' in their beer. He wanted to drown out the world in general, and women in particular.

The only thing standing in his way at the minute was a tall, shapely barmaid. He wanted her to bring him another beer, but she'd been cornered by a couple of mean drunks.

Chivalry's dead, he reminded himself, knowing full well that his inclinations toward gallantry usually led to trouble. On the other hand, there was nothing he despised more than a bully. Unless it was two very big bullies preying on one vulnerable woman.

Straightening a little from his slouched position in a corner booth, Ryan tipped back the brim of his Stetson with the long neck of his bottle. Eyes squinting against the thick haze of cigarette smoke, he watched as the no-account Turley brothers continued to harass one of Bubba's new barmaids.

Hank and Joe Turley were getting drunker by the minute, their language and gestures more foul with each drink. Seemed the brothers were determined to stir up a little action and they'd focused on the newcomer.

Ryan had been watching the same woman for a while, thinking she looked sorely out of place in here. Head high and spine straight, she moved with a dancer's grace. But her grace didn't conceal the fact that she was a rotten waitress.

She had that regal, touch-me-not air that piqued a man's interest, so she was getting more than her fair share of attention despite her sorry bartending skills.

He couldn't fault anyone for looking, though. She had a great figure and long, gorgeous legs. Her waitress uniform consisted of a snug white top, very short black skirt and spiked heels, which nicely displayed all her feminine assets.

His perusal included a leisurely glide up to her face. Pale, flawless skin stretched tight over a stubborn chin and high cheekbones. Her hair looked like dark cinnamon with a pile of curls at the back of her head. He couldn't see the color of her eyes, but they were big, wide-set and snapping with barely controlled temper as she dodged the badgering brothers.

So far, she'd been pretty good at evading their groping hands. If either of them reached for her again, they were asking for trouble. The way Ryan saw it, men were born to protect women, not prey on 'em. And any man who sat back and let it happen was equally spineless.

The thought sent a shot of adrenaline zinging through his veins, tightening his muscles as he anticipated a physical confrontation. Being outnumbered and outsized should have triggered caution, but not tonight.

An odd restlessness had been riding him for weeks now. He had a lot of pent-up frustration simmering inside him, adding fuel to his anger. When the Turleys blocked the swinging door, trapping the barmaid behind the counter, he was ready to fight.

Ryan took off his hat and set it on the chipped Formica of the table. He slowly uncoiled his long, hard length from the bench seat. Standing ramrod straight, he sauntered toward the bar, his jaw taut, eyes glittering with dark purpose.

He reached the trio in time to hear the waitress give the amorous brothers a firm, negative response to their bawdy invitations. Then Hank, the older one, grabbed her arm to hold her attention. The sight of the huge, grimy hand latching onto creamy pale skin sent a jolt of hot anger arcing through Ryan. He tensed even more, his fingers curling into fists.

"Hank. Joe." His tone was a low, menacing growl. "You both too dense to understand the meaning of the word 'no'?"

The big, beefy Turley brothers quickly turned their attention to him, interest in the waitress taking a backseat to his challenge. Their expressions were identically belligerent, the glazed gleam in their eyes turning ugly.

"Unless you're wantin' a serious whoopin' pretty boy, you'd best watch yer mouth," warned Hank, spokesman for the disgusting duo.

"Unless you're wantin' a serious whoopin'" Ryan mocked, "You'd better leave the lady alone." His demeanor was every bit as aggressive as theirs.

The brothers weren't used to being threatened. Their eyes narrowed as they turned more fully toward him, flexing muscles and puffing up their chests like banty roosters.

"Could be the lady's just playin' hard to get," Hank argued, his words a drunken slur.

Ryan knew better than to take his eyes off the brothers long enough to get assurances from the waitress. There wasn't an ounce of honor between the two of them, and he didn't relish the thought of being sucker punched.

The problem of the lady's mind-set was solved when he heard her mutter "Pigs".

He managed to keep a straight face, but mentally grinned at the disgust in her voice.

"Seems the lady knows your family," he taunted, and then watched Hank's face turn a fire-engine red. Joe was too dim-witted to catch the insult, but that didn't stop him from reacting to the challenge. Ryan braced himself when the big man came lunging at him, swinging his powerful right arm.

Grabbing the massive fist with both hands, he used Joe's forward momentum to twist him sharply sideways. Caught off balance, Joe stumbled. A swift kick in the rear shoved the big man into a nearby booth. He landed with a thud against Ted Branard's table, sending beer, glass, and tempers soaring.

Ted, a hothead himself, started cussing a blue streak. He and his three friends pounced on Joe, fists and vulgarities flying. Within seconds bodies were bouncing off nearby tables in a domino effect.

With Joe out of the way, Ryan had only to worry about Hank. As the second brother came rushing, he bent low and rammed his head into a rock-solid stomach. He heard a satisfying grunt of surprise, then felt a solid punch to his ribs that had him grunting as well.

The burst of pain pumped up more adrenaline, and he put all his strength behind an uppercut to Hank's chin. The crunch of bone on bone hurt him as much as his opponent, but it slammed the bigger man backward for an instant.

In his peripheral vision, Ryan saw Bubba come charging out of the kitchen, yelling and swearing, damning them all for destroying his property. In the space of a minute, total chaos had erupted. Glass was smashing and wood splintering. The music had stopped and nearly everyone in the bar was either fighting or cheering on someone who was fighting.

Hank came at him again, and Ryan took a couple punches to the chin and shoulder while landing a couple solid ones against the other man's rib cage. Someone slammed into them from another skirmish and sent them staggering sideways. Ryan landed against the bar, nearly face-to-face with the barmaid.

For just an instant, as he dragged in a harsh breath, he let himself be distracted by her expression. It held sheer disdain, and not a shred of encouragement. For some reason, that pleased him and prompted him to give her a grin.

She shook her head in disbelief, and then glanced behind him. "Watch out."

Ryan turned just in time to see Hank swinging a barstool at his head. He lifted an arm to ward off the attack and wood collided with bone in a teeth-jarring impact. Pain spiraled from his wrist to his shoulder, but there was no time to spare. The next attack came by way of a lethal splinter from the stool. Ryan dodged Hank's attempt to bury it in his gut and shoved him backward, sending him crashing against the bar.

As Hank paused to regain his balance, the barmaid lifted a fifth of whiskey and whacked him over the head with enough strength to stop him cold. The big drunk's eyes crossed and his expression distorted as he slowly slid to the floor.

"Damn," said Ryan, expelling the expletive with a rush of air. "You're good."

She frowned and leaned over the bar to study her unconscious victim. "Maybe I was a little too enthusiastic. I didn't mean to knock him out. Is he seriously hurt?"

Ryan grunted, leaning against the bar and fighting to catch his breath. "Are you kidding? It'd take more than a bottle to make a dent in that thick skull."

Touching the corner of his mouth, he felt the warmth of blood and the sting of a cut. Hank's punch to the left side of his face had done some damage. It was already sore and swelling. Luckily, his eyes and nose had been spared.

"Should I call 911?" asked the barmaid.

The question went unanswered as the strident sound of sirens pierced the clamor of the brawl. Ryan grimaced. No doubt Bubba had already called for help, and he didn't feel like dealing with the sheriff tonight. Now that his adrenaline was pumping, he felt more energized than he had in months. He didn't want to settle into respectability so soon.

The barmaid's big, heavily lashed eyes mirrored her consternation. Very bright, intelligent eyes, he thought as his breathing settled to a more natural rhythm. The mysterious lady had amazing green eyes. The expression in them revealed her displeasure at being caught in the middle of a brawl.

"How 'bout we slip out the back?" he said.

She hesitated a minute, shot a frowning glance at Bubba and decided to follow his suggestion. "This way."

Ryan stepped over Hank, around the bar and through the swinging door to the kitchen, leaving the worst of the noise and chaos behind him. The barmaid headed for the back door, but opened it to see the flashing red and blue lights of a sheriff's cruiser.

He heard a softly uttered curse as she slammed the door shut again. She turned and looked him straight in the eyes.

"Now what?"

"Is there a side door?" he asked.

Her eyes lit with relief and she nodded. "It's on the other side of the storage room and leads to the alley."

"Good." His mood was improving with every passing minute. Then he shifted his right arm and pain stabbed him. He clutched the injured hand, wondering if it was broken or just sprained.

He followed as she led the way to another exit, one that didn't have a patrol car parked outside. They both sighed in relief as they stepped outside and closed the door.

There was a nip in the spring air, but it felt good to Ryan's overheated body. He inhaled deeply, trying to clear the scent of stale cigarette smoke from his lungs. The adrenaline rush had cleared the beer buzz from his brain, but he still needed to wind down a little.

It was going on midnight. Streetlights were lit, but there was no activity and nobody in sight on this side of the building. They really did roll up the sidewalks in Kingston at dusk. Always had.

"Is your car in the front or out back?"

Ryan joined her as she peered around the building toward the entrance, glad he had driven one of the ranch work trucks tonight. For the moment, he relished playing the role of a down-on-his-luck cowboy.

"The black pickup," he said, nodding toward the well used, mud-spattered truck parked right next to the sheriff's cruiser.

"Drat," she whispered softly. "I was hoping you were just passing through town, but you're a local aren't you?"

"Yeah."

"Double drat. That means Bubba knows your truck. Even after the sheriff leaves, he'll be watching for you."

"Could be all night," he suggested smoothly, not in any hurry to part ways with her.

"You'll have to wait until he locks up and goes home. He can be really vile when he's in a temper, and any loss of profit can do that. After tonight's little fiasco, I don't imagine his disposition will improve for several days."

Ryan knew the cantankerous old barkeeper would bill him for every cent of damage and try to gouge him for more. He'd known that when he initiated the fight, but he didn't care.

"Do you live close?"

She turned more fully toward him. His eyes had adjusted to the darkness, so he studied her upturned face. Her features were more striking than beautiful with prominent cheekbones and a thin, straight nose. What she lacked in cosmetic beauty, though, she more than compensated with sex appeal. It oozed from every pore, kicking his libido into overdrive. His pulse had gradually settled, but now it drummed to a different beat.

Her eyes were clear and alive with intelligence, her lips full and beautifully shaped. Lips that gradually tightened into a disapproving line at his blatant perusal.

"In town or out?" she repeated impatiently.

Ryan wondered why she was so defensive. She'd been studying him just as closely, but he didn't suppose his looks were much of an asset right now. His eyes were bloodshot from lack of sleep, his face battered, his hair overdue for cutting, and he was sporting a couple days' worth of whisker stubble.

Besides, he'd just started a brawl. That in itself would stun the community and tarnish his reputation as an easygoing charmer. Of course, she wasn't privy to his reputation.

"My place is few miles out of town," he finally answered.

"Too far to walk home and come back for your truck later?"

"Way too far, but the truck doesn't matter much," he replied, "I couldn't drive it anyway."

Her gaze narrowed. "You've had too much to drink?"

He shook his head slightly, keeping his gaze locked with hers. "It's a standard."

"You mean it has a standard transmission?" she asked, brows knitting in a frown. "Why does that matter? If you drove it here then you obviously know how to handle a stick shift."

"I do," he replied, drawing out his explanation just to see how she reacted. Was she one of those no-nonsense people who always tempted him to tease?

"So," she snapped, not taking kindly to his deliberate manipulation. "Your point?"

The sparks in her eyes brought a twinkle to his. "So," he drawled with deliberate slowness. "I have to shift gears with my right hand, and I think mine's broken."

He liked the way her very kissable mouth rounded in distress. Her gaze dropped to the hand he was holding.

"Oh, no. Are you sure?"

"No." He was pretty sure, but hoping he was wrong.

Her frown deepened. "Well, hell."

Ryan chuckled softly. His mystery lady hadn't been prepared for the complication, and he had the feeling she wasn't the sort of woman who appreciated unexpected complications.

"How badly does it hurt?"

The grammatically correct question was uncommon to this area, so he tried to place her accent. It wasn't softly Southern, or crisp east coast. Somewhere in between, he reckoned, like an upper class midwestern.

"Are you in pain?" she asked again.

"Not much as long as I don't move it."

"Where's the nearest emergency room?"

"It's at the county hospital, a few miles south, but I can't go there. They'll take the other casualties to the emergency room and that'll be the sheriff's next stop."

"What then? You're just going to hope it's not serious? What if it's broken and starts swelling? Or starts to heal improperly? Won't they have to re-break it or something?"

"Well," he answered slowly, thinking out loud, "there's a doctor in town who doesn't mind the occasional house call."

"And just how can he make a house call if you're not at your house?" she demanded, crossing her arms over her chest, her body language shouting impatience with his laid-back attitude.

This time the chuckle escaped along with Ryan's grin. "He has an office in his home, so he takes calls there."

"At midnight?"

"All hours of the day and night."

She didn't look convinced, but she stopped arguing. "How close does he live? Within walking distance?"

"It's on the other end of town."

"Then we're back to square one."

"How about your car?" he asked, glancing to the parking lot where the cruiser's lights illuminated several vehicles.

"I walked."

That surprised him. Bubba's was on the far north end of town and most of the residential areas were on the south side. The only place close was a fleabag motel.

"Then you either have a really long walk to work or you're living in a real dive," he said flatly.

That put her shoulders back and brought her chin up sharply. Her eyes glittered like emerald fire in the darkness.

"Where I live and how far I walk to work are none of your business. And if you were better at minding your own business, you wouldn't have a broken arm in the first place."

Ryan frowned. Wanting to be sure he understood what she meant, he asked, "You don't think I should have interfered between you and the Turleys?"

"Right first time, cowboy."

"That's gratitude for you. I'm injured trying to rescue a damsel in distress, and I'm the one getting harassed."

"Just for the record," she enunciated very clearly, her expression long-suffering. "I was not in need of rescuing."

"Sure looked like it to me."

"Then your vision is seriously impaired. If I'd been in trouble, I would have called Bubba to intervene. I was trying to avoid the confrontation you so zealously initiated."

"That so?" he drawled, his pride stinging.

"That's so."

"I suppose that means you don't owe me your life or even a favor?" His tone echoed with disappointment.

She rolled her eyes and sighed, brushing a wayward curl off her cheek. Ryan's gaze followed the action, and he found himself fascinated by the silken smoothness of her skin. He had a sudden yearning to touch it and test its warmth and softness.

"I don't owe you a thing, but I guess it's my humanitarian duty to see that you get some medical attention. Are you sure there's a doctor who'll see you tonight?"

"If he's home, he'll see me."

"Then we'll have to go get my car," she said, turning from him and heading down the alley. He didn't know if his mystery lady made a habit of trekking down alleys, but she didn't hesitate, so neither did he.

"You're living at the Sweet Dreams Motel?"

"That's what the sign says."

It hurt his mouth to grin, but he couldn't resist. His new friend had a wicked sense of humor.

"I won't even be able to afford that if Bubba blames me for tonight's debacle and fires me," she grumbled.

He didn't like the sound of that. It stung his pride even more and troubled his sense of justice. He'd meant to help, not hurt her, but he wouldn't put anything past the irascible old bartender. There had to be a way to right the wrong.

"What will you do? Have any friends or family in town?"

She ignored his probing questions and kept walking. "I'll have to wait and see how Bubba reacts. Or maybe I can find another job in town."

"Doubtful," said Ryan, dodging a trash receptacle. He'd been so engrossed in the sassy sway of her hips that he hadn't noticed the dumpster.

She stopped until he caught up with her again. "Why is it doubtful?"

"Because Bubba's family owns half the businesses in Kingston."

"Thus Bubba's Bar and Gary's Garage. I'm familiar with a couple of them. Obviously they're a family strong on originality. Any other relatives to avoid?"

"Well." He tried to keep a rein on his amusement. "If I were you, I wouldn't apply for a job at Sandy's Salon or Granny's Gun Shop."

The alley dead-ended into the motel's parking lot. She turned to confront him, hands on hips.

Her tone was indignant. "You're making that up!"

Laughter rumbled from Ryan's chest. "Scout's honor," he swore. She didn't ask if he'd ever been a scout. She just shook her head in disbelief, and then headed across the parking lot.

"Are we going to your room?" Ryan asked hopefully. His stomach muscles tightened at the thought of tumbling into bed with her.

"Don't push your luck," she warned. "I'm under no obligation to get you to a doctor. I might still decide that you're more trouble than you're worth."

Ryan's low, husky laughter filled the night air. His wrist hurt like hell. He was bruised and bleeding with various parts of his body throbbing in pain or protest, but he couldn't remember the last time he'd felt like laughing.

*****

Erica wove through parked cars and passed through a breezeway that divided the building, then turned to be sure her quixotic cowboy had followed. The last thing in the world she needed right now was involvement with a man, so she didn't welcome the tug of attraction as she watched him slowly ambling toward her.

It should be against the law for a man to wear jeans that clung so lovingly to long legs, muscled thighs and slim hips.

The sight of him sent shivers along her nerves. She shook her head to rid it of lascivious thoughts.

"My car's parked back here," she explained, taking the lead again as they rounded the building.

The lighting was minimal, yet she wasn't afraid of the darkness. The crime rate in her temporary home was near zero. Years of parental warnings and caution weren't totally discarded, but she felt safe with her wounded stranger.

"I just realized that I don't even know your name."

For years, it had been a professional habit to offer her hand along with short, crisp introductions. It seemed strange to ask for his name, reminding her of how far from home and her normal life she'd drifted.

"Ryan."

Erica's brows creased. The man had been flirting shamelessly with her for the past half hour, and all he was willing to supply was a first name? Was he trying to hide something? Why? She wasn't likely to recognize his name even if he was the local bad boy and had a horrible reputation.

For some totally incomprehensible reason, his slight snub stung. She wasn't pleased with her own reaction, and her annoyance gave way to perversity. She didn't offer her own name until he asked for it.

"And you are?"

Two could play the game. "Erica."

"Nice to meet you, Erica," he replied.

The thread of amusement in his tone created another little quiver of response in her. The man was a menace. She knew his type, smooth and handsome and used to having his way with woman. The type she'd always made a point to avoid.

Of course, her current situation was anything but normal. In fact, her life had gone to hell. One minute she'd been an ambitious, upwardly mobile executive and then wham! She'd been bypassed for a promotion. It had scrambled her emotions and maybe even her common sense. It had made her take a long, hard look at her life and realize how much it sucked.

At the ripe old age of twenty-six, she'd suffered some sort of life crisis. She'd suddenly realized that all she had to show for years of study, hard work and single-minded dedication was a stalled career and no personal life.

All her closest friends were married and having babies. The nesting instinct had bypassed her. She wasn't involved in a serious relationship, and her non-serious one was with a man who dated her to get closer to her family fortune. She didn't even have an adoring pet.

She'd never made time for hobbies, she didn't know how to play or even relate to people who did know how to play. She might be a dynamo in the corporate world, but as a person, she'd be lucky to rate a five on a scale of one to ten. It was damned depressing, thought Erica, as they reached her car.

The large relic had been purchased from a used car lot for a few hundred dollars. She pulled the keys out of her pocket, unlocked and opened the driver's door. Then she slid behind the wheel and leaned over to unlock the passenger door.

"You must be the only person in Kingston who locks their car," said Ryan as he carefully eased into his side of the front seat and pulled the door shut with his good hand.

"Force of habit."

Erica turned the ignition, and then waited until the engine fired, sputtered and died. She pumped the gas and tried again, having learned that this boat of a car never started on the first try. It was a nuisance, but one she could live with temporarily.

She gave her passenger points for not criticizing her mode of transportation. It was big and ugly, but dependable. The price had been reasonable, too, and she'd needed space to haul around her belongings. Her sleek, expensive sports car wouldn't have been practical for Wyoming.

"Where to?"

Ryan gave her directions, and then offered tidbits of information about the town and its businesses as they drove the nearly deserted streets. Once they'd gotten to the residential area, he directed her to an affluent neighborhood. They turned into a cul-de-sac, and he pointed out the one house that still had lights blazing.

"Looks like the doctor might be entertaining," she said, pulling to a stop at the curb.

"He's not much of a party animal."

Erica shrugged and shut off the engine. Ryan climbed from the car, slammed the door and headed up the sidewalk. As an apparent afterthought, he motioned for her.

She hesitated, but decided she might as well follow him. She was curious to meet the doctor and see how he'd react to their unexpected visit. Besides, setting a broken bone could take a while, and she had no desire to wait alone in the car.

Chapter Two

Ryan bypassed the front of the house and circled around to a side door where the windows were dark. He was ringing the bell as Erica approached. She noticed a small plaque that read, "Ned Grayson, MD".

In a matter of minutes, a light came on and the inside door swung open. An attractive, dark-haired man of medium height and build greeted them with obvious surprise.

"Ryan, what the heck?"

"Hi, Doc. Sorry to just show up on your doorstep, but I was hoping you might be hard up for business."

The doctor shook his head in disbelief, but pushed the storm door wide to invite them into his office.

Once he got a good look at Ryan in the light, he frowned. "Can't say I'm desperate for patients, but you look worse for wear. What happened?"

"A little brawl at Bubba's."

Their host's eyes widened in amazement. He gave Ryan a long, probing look, then his gaze swung to her. She accepted his swift, professional assessment without offense. Instead of dismissing her for her tacky outfit or barmaid status, he smiled with respect and appreciation.

She liked him already.

"How about an introduction?" he asked Ryan.

Professionalism she could understand. Erica stepped forward and offered her hand, feeling more comfortable than she had in weeks. "Erica Smyth, and I assume you're Dr. Grayson."

"Right first try," he teased, giving her hand a firm, warm shake. "Most people just call me Doc."

She offered him a smile. "It's a pleasure to meet you, Doc. My apologies for the unannounced visit."

"No problem," he assured, "but tell me, what's a lovely lady like you doing working at a place like Bubba's? Writing a thesis on honky-tonks? Working undercover for the FBI?"

Her smile widened, and she gave him extra points for effort. She was pleased at his perceptiveness. Despite her best efforts, she'd been a miserable failure at tending bar.

"Just trying to earn a living."

Ryan loudly cleared his throat. "I'm in pain here," he reminded testily.

Erica and the doctor shared a grin, and then turned their attention back to the patient.

"Where does it hurt the worst?" asked Doc.

Ryan lifted his right arm. "My hand."

"Broken?"

"Probably."

Doc took hold of his wrist and examined it. "I'll have to take some x-rays. Anything else get cracked too hard? Ribs?"

"Just a little bruised, I think. Old Hank did a number on my wrist with a barstool."

"Hank Turley? That means Joe had to be in on the fracas. How come you tangled with those two?"

"Oh, Ryan didn't just tangle with them," supplied Erica, "he challenged them to a duel."

Doc's brows creased as he looked to him for confirmation. "Just in the mood to fight?" he asked, his tone bland.

Ryan scowled. "Maybe I was just doing a good deed."

The doctor snorted, not disguising his skepticism, and Ryan's expression grew mutinous. Erica shifted her gaze from one to the other, sensing more behind the doctor's question than the obvious. Curiosity piqued, she wondered what ulterior motive Ryan might have had for starting a brawl.

"If you'll excuse us for a minute, Erica, I need to take Superman into the x-ray closet. We won't be long, so please make yourself comfortable."

"Thank you, but what I'd really like is to use the bathroom. Do you mind?"

Doc shook his head. "Not at all. Right over there," he said, pointing to a door on the left side of room. He led Ryan toward a door on the opposite side of the small clinic.

Erica scrubbed her hands and then glanced in the mirror. She was looking pretty frayed around the edges, but there wasn't much she could do about it. She smoothed a few errant curls back into her barrette, splashed water on her face and wiped it dry.

There was nothing she could do about the foul smell of grease and smoke clinging to her clothes and hair. She'd never realized that a person absorbed that kind of strong odor. It was the most disgusting thing about her job. Most days, even more disgusting than customers like the Turleys. By the end of her shift, she was desperate for a shower. Just like now.

The men were back in the main office when she opened the door. Erica felt the sudden heaviness of tension between them. She wished she knew what they'd been discussing. All she'd caught of their conversation was the name Katlyn. Ryan's girlfriend? An ex-wife? A current wife or girlfriend?

Why did it matter? Why did the mention of some unknown woman make her teeth clench? She shook her head in disgust and forced herself to relax. Ryan was nothing to her. She knew nothing about him and didn't plan to get involved. Reminding herself about curiosity killing the cat, she firmly closed the bathroom door. The men's conversation abruptly ended.

"So what's the diagnosis?" she asked, glancing toward the x-ray they were both studying.

"Well, there's a hairline fracture right here between the little finger and wrist," Doc said, pointing to a tiny line on the x-ray. "It's not bad as breaks go, but it'll have to be in a cast for about six weeks."

Ryan mumbled a string of oaths. "Can't you just put a bandage on it or put it in a sling for a while?"

"Best I can do is a cast that won't totally immobilize your fingers. It'll take me a minute to get ready if you want to clean up first. Afterward, you can't get the cast wet."

Ryan glanced down at his bloodstained shirt. "Got something clean I can borrow?"

"Spare shirts in the bathroom cabinet. Help yourself."

Ryan left the room, returning a few minutes later, hair damp, his face and arms scrubbed clean. He'd changed from a long-sleeved shirt to a short-sleeved T-shirt that was just a little snug. The soft black fabric emphasized a well-developed upper body that narrowed to an impossibly flat stomach.

Something about the haphazard way he tucked the shirttail into his jeans made Erica's stomach muscles knot, unfurling a heated response over the rest of her body. The unexpected, unwelcome pull of attraction had her swiftly averting her gaze and chastising herself for the typically feminine response.

She'd never been the type who swooned over hunk material. A man's intelligence and personality usually impressed her more than his physical attributes. Her very physical response to the rogue cowboy was alarming as well as annoying. She attributed it to fatigue and their bizarre circumstances.

Ryan sat on the edge of an examination table. She took a seat and watched as Doc deftly applied the cast. In a few minutes, they were ready to leave.

"This shouldn't give you a lot of pain unless you try to do too much too soon," said Doc. The cast covered Ryan's right arm from his palm to his forearm, leaving him limited motion in his fingers, but immobilizing his wrist.

"What's too much and too soon?" he asked.

"Give it a week or two before you start slinging it around, and then take it slow."

"I'm right-handed, Doc."

"Well, this is a good time to learn how to use your left."

"And until I learn?"

"You'll need help. Anyone out at your place right now?"

"No."

Doc frowned and glanced at Erica. "Ever had any aspirations to join the nursing profession?"

She shook her head in quick dismissal of the idea. "Not even a little bit, and I already have a job."

"Had a job," Ryan reminded.

She grimaced. He was right, of course. Bubba had already threatened to fire her twice in the past three weeks. He'd never let her keep working now. He owed her a week's pay, but he could withhold her final paycheck. If so, she'd be broke. Even the fleabag motel would be out of her price range.

"Are you planning to stay with Ryan the rest of the night?" asked Doc. "I want to give him some medication for pain and muscle spasms, but he shouldn't drive or be alone."

Erica's eyes widened. Doc assumed they were a couple, and that she'd be willing to play nursemaid. She prided herself in being a good judge of character, and thought both these men were decent people, but she didn't know either of them well.

Her gaze clashed with Ryan's. "Don't you have a family? A wife or a girlfriend?"

He slowly shook his head, never breaking eye contact. He had such beautiful eyes, she mused, momentarily distracted. They were bruised and bloodshot, but still mesmerizing enough to make her lose her train of thought. A long, breathless moment later, she snapped back to attention.

"Surely you have some friends!"

"Plenty, but none that I want to drag out of their beds at this time of night."

Erica's frown deepened. Her growing fascination with Ryan was getting more complex by the minute. She didn't welcome the tug of sexual attraction, so she needed to be extra cautious.

"I don't even know your last name," she challenged.

"Havens." The men chorused in unison and watched her expectantly.

He didn't look much like a cocky cowboy right now, just a man who was battered and exhausted. She wondered how long it had been since he'd slept. He looked ready to collapse. She didn't want to care, but the feeling just sneaked up on her.

"I'd offer you a bed," Doc injected, "but Tammy's having her very first sleepover. More than a dozen giggling, energetic seven-year-olds. There'll be no peace here tonight."

Erica smiled at his long-suffering tone. A slumber party explained why the house was still lit up at such a late hour.

"Thanks, Doc, but I'll get by."

"How about you, Erica? Live anywhere nearby?"

"The motel," Ryan answered for her.

Doc didn't try to hide his shock. "Alone?"

She sighed. She wouldn't be staying there tonight. Her meager tips wouldn't stretch far enough for another night at the motel. Without a paycheck, she'd be sleeping in her car.

"Why don't you go home with Ryan? He needs a little extra help, and he's got plenty of room at his place. It'll be a lot safer than the motel."

Erica's brows puckered at the suggestion, her gaze locking with Ryan's. She could tell that he approved of the suggestion, but could he be trusted? She assumed the good-natured doctor was a reliable reference. The Harvard Medical School diploma on his wall seemed legitimate, and he seemed sincere. It wouldn't be that risky to drive Ryan home. He didn't look like much of a threat and would be even less after he'd taken some medication.

Exhaustion was settling over her, too. She was used to spending twelve hours a day in high heels, but not while hefting twenty-pound serving trays. Every muscle in her body ached with fatigue. Her sinuses throbbed from too many hours of too little fresh air. She wanted get out of her work clothes and shower away the stink of the bar.

Not one to dally over decisions, she said. "I guess I can drive you home and help you get settled." If she didn't like the looks of the place, she could always head back to town.

"That's probably best, and I promise you can trust him with your life," said Doc.

Her life wasn't endangered, thought Erica, just her peace of mind. But the doctor's words were reassuring.

"We can discuss details on the way," said Ryan.

"All right," she said, slowly rising from her seat.

Doc gave Ryan a couple of pills and a glass of water to swallow them. Then he handed her the pill bottle and directions on the care of the cast. He saw them to the door, and shrugged off their thanks.

"Let me know what I owe you."

"Don't worry, you'll get my bill. Anything after midnight is time and a half, you know."

"I got no quarrel with that." The amicable response was testimony to Ryan's weariness. "Much obliged."

After exchanging good-byes, they left the house, and Doc closed the door behind them. The night had grown colder, so Erica hurried to the car and went through the starting ritual while Ryan made his way more slowly down the sidewalk.

Even though she suffered a few guilt pangs, it wasn't really her fault he was tired and hurting. She hadn't asked him to play the conquering hero. The offer to drive him home was more than generous under the circumstances.

The streetlight illuminated Ryan's features as he eased himself into the car. Despite his five o'clock shadow and darkening bruises, he really was a gorgeous specimen. What woman wouldn't be enticed by thick, wavy blond hair, the blinding blue of his eyes and the rugged beauty of his high, strong cheekbones? Not to mention the cleft in his chin that was a temptation in itself.

She had absolutely no experience in picking up strange men in bars, nor did she want any, but she supposed most women would consider her guest quite a trophy.

Ryan glanced at her. "What?" he asked.

Embarrassed to be caught staring, she said the first thing that popped into her mind. "It just dawned on me that I've joined the ranks of women who pick up strange men in bars."

His eyes glittered with amusement. "First time, huh?"

"First and last." Her tone was adamant. She shook off the niggling sizzle of attraction and followed his directions.

They stopped by the motel long enough to gather her things. After that, it took less than fifteen minutes to reach their destination. The ranch had a mile-long driveway bordered by rows and rows of wooden fences. Darkness prevented Erica from seeing the whole property, but the place looked huge, making her parents' large Chicago estate seem small in comparison.

Security lights illuminated several big barns and other outbuildings. The main house was a rambling three-story structure with a wraparound porch.

"Where should I park? Where do you live?"

"Park near the back door." He pointed the way. "I'm the manager, and I live in the house."

"Alone?"

"When the owners are gone. Which is 98 percent of the year."

"How big is the whole operation?"

"About seventy thousand acres, but some is in federal rest."

"How big is the staff?"

"Five full-timers and ten helping with spring chores."

"Do any of them live on the property?"

"A few share the bunk house. The foreman has his own place. Two regulars are married and live nearby. Most of the part-timers are transients or teenagers who work after school."

She pulled to a stop, shifted to park and shut off the ignition. They were both quiet as they considered the next course of action. Even though she'd said she'd help him tonight, Erica wondered if one of his staff could do it. She looked at the darkened house and remembered every horror story she'd ever heard about strangers.

Then Ryan turned to make her an offer.

"Look, I know it's not practical to spend the night with a stranger, but our situation is unusual at best. We're both exhausted. I'm battered. This is the ranch's busy season, and help is hard to find. I can offer you a job that includes room and board. I promise you it's above and beyond anything Bubba or the Sweet Dreams can offer, but you'll have to trust me."

Erica didn't think anything could be worse than Bubba's and the motel, but she was still wary. "What type of job? I don't know anything about ranching."

"Are you looking for short-term work or long-term?"

"Short-term."

"How short?"

"Three weeks."

"Why three weeks?"

"Just because." She didn't offer any personal details.

Ryan stared at her intently. "Can you cook?"

She shifted her gaze from the intensity of his and lifted her right hand, wiggling the fingers. "I'm pretty good with the buttons on a microwave."

"How about computers? Know anything about them?"

"I have great computer skills."

"Any accounting skills?"

"Enough to read a spreadsheet, but probably not enough to create one. Why are you asking?"

"What I need is someone willing to combine light housekeeping with a little secretarial work."

Erica's brows creased. "I told you I can't cook. At least nothing fancy and certainly not for large groups." She didn't mention that she'd never done any housekeeping in her life. "But I am dependable and hardworking."

"That sounds good to me. You're hired if you want the job. I can give you an advance if you want to stay at the motel, but this is a big house. You'd have plenty of space and privacy when you're not working."

Erica bit her lip. Decision time. Common sense told her to drop Ryan off and be on her way. That would be the smartest, most sensible thing to do. Until three weeks ago, she'd never done anything that wasn't smart or practical or at least necessary. But something deep inside urged her to take a chance, to make the most of the brief interlude of freedom.

A shudder raced over her at the thought of another night in that motel. She hadn't gotten a good night's sleep for weeks. The doctor had given Ryan an excellent character reference, and she trusted the cowboy to keep his word.

"What's it gonna be?" he asked. "Willing to take a chance on the unknown? Or would you rather keep running?"

Erica shot him an irritated glance. "I'm not running from anything or anybody. I'm too tired to face the drive back to town. I'll accept the job with room and board, but I reserve the right to leave whenever I see fit."

"Fair enough. It's a deal."

With that, her passenger opened his door and carefully eased his long, lean body from the car. Erica climbed out, too, then collected her purse and overnight bag. She followed slowly as Ryan approached the house. Then he opened a door and held it for her to enter.

They walked directly into a long, wide kitchen. He switched on a light, illuminating a room decorated in sunshine yellow with white appliances and hardwood furniture and cupboards. Everything looked clean and shining, a huge improvement over Bubba's and the motel.

Ryan walked through the kitchen and into an office with the usual furnishings—wooden file cabinets, a couple of easy chairs, a big oak desk complete with a computer, printer and fax machine. He slowly settled into a leather recliner and even more slowly tilted it backward into a reclining position.

"Here's where I'm spending the rest of the night," he mumbled as he closed his eyes and sighed. Lifting an arm, he pointed to the doorway on the opposite side of the room. "You can use that bedroom and bath. I'll show you the rest of the house tomorrow and you can have your pick of guest rooms."

Erica considered herself dismissed, but she watched as he toed off his boots. They hit the floor with a thud and another deep sigh. His dark gold lashes drifted over his cheeks and his breathing settled to an even rhythm. She spent another few minutes studying his ruggedly handsome features and wondering about his effect on her hormones.

She didn't want to feel any attraction, yet she didn't know how to combat the chemistry. Never having met a man who stirred her senses so strongly, her reactions left her feeling unprepared and exposed. From the minute he'd looked into her eyes, she'd felt a fierce connection. A zing of awareness coupled with a camaraderie that was totally alien to her.

She wasn't looking for a romantic relationship. That was the last thing she needed right now, yet she couldn't imagine just walking away and never seeing him again.

The last thing she needed was a charming flirt who deemed himself a knight in armor. She considered herself a good judge of character, but he didn't fit any of the usual stereotypes. On one hand he seemed intelligent and honorable. On the other hand, he downed beer in bars and started brawls. It didn't make sense. What kind of man started a free-for-all and enjoyed every minute of it? Certainly not the type she normally dated.

She was bone-deep tired, both in body and spirit. Was it worth it? The question kept replaying in her mind. Three weeks ago she hadn't had a doubt in her mind. As time passed, the doubts plagued her.

When she'd left home, she'd taken a six-week leave of absence from the family firm. There was no way she'd return to Chicago a day early, but her personal credit card was maxed. She needed to support herself for three more weeks.

After years of dedicating twelve-hour days and six-day weeks to the family business, Erica had been devastated when her dad chose another executive for promotion. Especially since Geoffrey had frequently taken credit for her work and lied about his rapport with their clients.

Shaking her head at the memory, she shrugged off worries about the company and carried her bags to the bathroom. Within fifteen minutes, she'd showered and readied for bed.

One last thought of Ryan had her pulling a blanket from the bed and carrying it back to the office.

* * * * *

Ryan didn't know whether he'd slept a few minutes or an hour. The ache in his broken hand was subsiding, but taking a deep breath still induced pain. The left side of his face was stiff, making him wonder if he had a bruised jaw and black eye. The knuckles on both his hands were sore and starting to throb.

A totally different part of his body developed an ache as he watched Erica move back into the room. She wore a short, thin nightshirt and carried a blanket in front of her, frustrating him with a too-narrow view of sleek, bare legs.

With her came a rush of moist, sweetly scented air. His body tightened in response. He was physically drained, but he figured a man would have to be dead not to react to the sight and smell of such an incredibly sexy woman. Her shirt was simple yellow cotton. It wasn't provocative, but the way it clung to her curves made his pulse hum with excitement.

And the way she moved. Her slow, graceful glide across the room fascinated him. She'd washed her hair. It was damp and shining and fell sleekly to her shoulders, the weight of it subduing the thick curls into sensuous waves. He wanted to sink his fingers in it and feel the silky texture.

He wanted to feel all of her, every single inch from the top of her damp head to the tip of her toes. Desire slammed through him, hotter and harder than he'd felt in months. Ryan groaned, a low sound of self-disgust. He actually wanted a woman with shocking force, and there was no way he was going to get what he wanted and needed tonight. Damn his luck.

He didn't need complications in his life. Didn't want emotional involvement. Physical involvement held great appeal, but his mystery lady wasn't offering. His body sang with pleasure as he watched Erica come toward him. Gone was the brassy barmaid. She'd metamorphosed into the stuff dreams were made of, all soft and sexy and feminine.

When she moved closer to his chair, her sweet, clean scent enveloped him. Then she leaned over him.

Ryan kept his eyes partially shuttered as his gaze roamed from her narrow waist to the lush curves of her breasts. Their fullness pressed against the softness of her nightshirt, causing blood to rush to his loins. Silently cursing, he fought to control the violent, unexpected surge of need.

He didn't need any more frustration in his life. But damn, she looked and smelled so good, and he was so needy.

Chapter Three

Erica touched the back of her hand to Ryan's forehead. He reached up to grasp it in his own, surprising them both by slowly drawing it to his mouth and placing a kiss in her palm.

"Hi."

His one little word was rich with warmth and pleasure. It caused a ripple of reaction through Erica. She couldn't remember ever being so strongly affected by something so basic as the deep, welcoming tone of a man's voice.

"Hi yourself, cowboy. Are you in pain? You were mumbling or grumbling. I'm not sure which."

"Dreaming," he clarified, lifting his good hand to gently stroke her cheek with his thumb. "Dreaming about slow, sweet kisses from a pretty nurse."

Her heart lurched, sending her pulse racing like a scared rabbit. The gentle stroke of his callused fingers sent a heated shimmer of need through her. The temptation to give him what he wanted was shocking, thrilling and dangerous.

"Too bad there aren't any pretty nurses around."

"Too bad," he agreed, but the sleepy smile on his battered face was without regret. "Kiss me."

Her breath got trapped in her lungs, then her throat. The man was certifiable, brash and insolent. His mouth looked swollen and sore. He had no business kissing anyone, and yet she couldn't remember ever hungering for a kiss so badly.

She leaned closer to cover him with the blanket, and he slid his good arm around her waist. His strength caught her off guard as he lifted her and pulled her across his body. She gasped in shock. Dropping the blanket, she planted both hands against his chest.

"Ryan!" Erica yelped in surprise. She struggled briefly, but went still when he moaned in pain. "You're insane!"

"I had to bring you closer because I'm not moving too well," he said, his eyes glinting with challenge.

Her nightshirt rode up her hips, leaving her thighs bare. The denim of his jeans did little to disguise his arousal, but he didn't steal a kiss or take advantage of her vulnerable position. He just waited. Erica knew he wanted her to make the next move. He wanted her to prove she was equally involved.

It was a mistake to further complicate their relationship. Her analytical mind knew it for a fact. Her practical nature urged her to refuse him. Her sense of self-preservation warned her to back off even as she lowered her head that final inch.

Their lips barely touched, gently brushing in sensual exploration. The kiss was as soft as a rose petal, yet Erica felt it to the tips of her toes. When his tongue flirted with her mouth, seeking entrance, her toes curled. Parting her lips, she welcomed the probing warmth of his tongue, then sucked it ever so gently into her mouth. A low moan erupted from Ryan's throat, but she knew this one wasn't from pain.

They kissed until there was no more breath in their lungs, and then he withdrew his tongue from her mouth and coaxed hers into his. She flicked it across his teeth and the inside of his cheeks, teasing until he began to suck it more hungrily.

Erica sank both her hands into the thickness of his hair as their mouths parted again. They stared at each other for a few pulsing heartbeats, then he stole another long, deep kiss.

Her nipples tingled and hardened, poking against his chest, and she began to ache for more.

The rock-hard strength of his erection pressed against the cradle of her thighs, making her body throb with an answering arousal. Her muscles turned to putty and her resistance began to falter. The heat he ignited in her burned deep and hot.

She'd never been aroused so swiftly and with no more enticement than a man's hypnotic charm and tender kisses. The sheer strength of her reaction increased her sensual alarm and had her withdrawing, gradually easing space between them.

A look of regret flashed in his eyes as he loosened his hold on her. She stared down at him, worrying her bottom lip with her teeth. The rapidly escalating attraction between them could disrupt any plans to work together.

"We don't need this kind of complication," she insisted, her voice husky.

Ryan didn't respond, just continued to look at her with a come-hither gleam in his eyes. His wordless seduction was nearly as irresistible as his kisses. Damn, but the man had beautiful, expressive eyes.

Pushing away from him with her hands and clearing her throat, she tried to sound firm. "If your job offer includes sex, then you'd better clarify your intent right now."

He returned her steady gaze. "I'm not expecting sexual favors if you work for me. The employment arrangement is strictly business."

"You swear?"

"I swear I'm not going to pressure you for sex, but I'm damned sure not going to refuse it if it's offered," he said.

She nodded, accepting his word because he was an honorable man. She wasn't sure why she knew that, but she did.

Still trembling, she slowly eased herself from his body and off the chair, immediately missing his warmth and hardness. "I'd like to accept the job offer, but I'm not offering a sexual relationship in return."

He didn't try to hold her against her will. She wondered if he'd be furious at her withdrawal and consider her a tease.

Instead, she watched as a gleam of mischief entered his eyes.

"Then I don't suppose you're interested in a wildly passionate, totally torrid one-night stand, are you?"

She found the suggestion so appealing that she had to lie and chastise him. "No, I'm not, and who do you think you're kidding? You're so battered you can hardly move."

Ryan argued, but his tone wasn't much stronger than the rest of him. "I could do it just fine with a little help."

She shook her head in disbelief. "Forget it, cowboy, and don't try any more funny business. If you give me more trouble, you'll be sorry."

"How's that?" he challenged drowsily.

"I have a black belt in karate, and I can make you hurt in more places than you ever imagined," she warned.

The tone she intended to be firm turned into a mixture of tenderness and rebuke. A grin split the swollen tightness of his face. "There's no place left that doesn't hurt."

Erica knew he was fighting to keep his eyes open, but apparently the medicine kicked in, and he abruptly fell asleep. She intended to do the same.

After covering him with the blanket, she headed back to the bedroom. As she crawled beneath the covers of the king-sized bed, Ryan's scent enveloped her. A low whimper escaped as she realized he'd given her his bed.

* * * * *

When Erica woke, daylight was shining brightly through the bedroom window. She slowly stretched and glanced around her, searching for a clock. She located one on the bedside stand and realized it was almost noon.

It amazed her that she'd slept so long and felt so rested. Despite being submerged in Ryan's scent, or maybe because of it, she'd slept soundly all night. She hadn't done that any other night since leaving Chicago.

She'd never really lived alone. During college she'd had roommates. After graduation she'd moved back to her parents' home. It was just more practical. Her main interest had always been the business, so she'd gratefully left the cleaning, cooking and laundry chores to their household staff.

Living alone these past few weeks had caused her a lot of sleepless nights. She wasn't afraid while she was awake and fully clothed, but it was different at night. Being alone in a strange room in a strange town hadn't been very conducive to restful sleep. Alone in bed, she'd felt especially vulnerable.

Having a man nearby, even a wounded one, made her feel safer. At least subconsciously. What a disconcerting reality, thought Erica, hating to admit the fact. She never wanted to be dependent on a man for her basic needs. Still, she was thankful for the good night's sleep.

The aroma of freshly brewed coffee teased her senses, so she slipped out of bed and into the bathroom. After washing her face and brushing her teeth, she dressed in a pale lavender sweat suit. A glance in the mirror revealed the usual tangle of wayward curls. She brushed them severely and clipped her hair back in a plastic claw fastener, then went in search of caffeine.

Ryan had his back to her when she entered the kitchen. He stood at the counter, trying to pour a cup of coffee, but making a mess of it. Erica noticed how awkward he was with his left hand and gently pushed him aside.

"Sit down. I'll pour the coffee."

"Thanks." He slowly eased himself into a chair.

"You're not looking too frisky this morning," she commented as she joined him at the table.

The left side of his face was turning a colorful black and blue. There was a split in his upper lip, his left eye was nearly swollen shut, and he needed a shave. His hair was rumpled, his expression pained. He didn't appear to be moving well, either.

"I've had better days," was his only reply.

"And better weeks?" she asked.

"Better weeks," he conceded, but his eyes glittered challengingly. "I'm guessing you've had better, too."

"I've had a lot of new experiences lately."

"Like participating in a brawl, dodging the law, picking up a man in the bar and losing your job?"

She scowled at him. "It wasn't much of a job, and I wasn't very good at it, but I didn't want to lose it."

"Tending bar at Bubba's is the only job you've ever had?"

She frowned at the suggestion. "I've worked ever since I was a teenager, but I'm not in a position to supply references, so it was all I could get."

"Why no references? You must not be an embezzler or you wouldn't need to work. At least not a very successful one. I can't think of any other reason you wouldn't want to list a former employer," said Ryan.

"There are other reasons for leaving a position besides embezzlement," she argued.

"Burn your bridges behind you?" he taunted.

She chose to take a sip of coffee rather than comment.

"Corporate espionage? You tampered with the company books? You're facing litigation?" Ryan offered a list of possibilities. "You had an affair with the boss?"

"You're being rude and incredibly narrow-minded. I could have chosen to leave the firm for reasons that are neither illegal nor immoral. Why assume I've done something wrong?"

"Because you're so secretive about it. You haven't shared any personal information since we met. Most women give me their life story within minutes of meeting."

"Then you're meeting the wrong women," she insisted.

Ryan frowned at her, but their conversation was interrupted by a brief knock at the door. He called "come in" and two cowboys joined them in the kitchen. One was tall and lean and about Ryan's age, the other older, shorter and stocky. They hesitated when they saw Erica.

Ryan made the introductions. "Erica, this is the ranch foreman, Zack Draper," he said of the younger man, "and our blacksmith, Will Saunders. Zack, Will, this is Erica Smyth."

Both men tipped their hats. That seemed to be the standard form of greeting, so she accepted it with a smile. Their expressions were curious, but respectful. They probably knew she was involved with the fiasco at Bubba's, yet they didn't seem to hold it against her.

"It's nice to meet you."

"Pleasure, ma'am," they chorused.

Zack turned his attention to Ryan. "We heard you got into a little scrape at Bubba's last night."

"How'd you bust your arm?" asked Will.

"Hank Turley whacked it with a barstool," Ryan explained, holding up the cast.

The men shook their heads in commiseration.

"We made a trip to town to see if you needed some help, but couldn't find hide nor hair of ya," said the older man.

"Heard ya taught those Turleys a lesson, but Bubba sure was fired up."

"Erica saved me from Bubba's wrath," he explained. "She took me to Doc's, then drove me home. I've hired her to help for the next few weeks."

Neither of the men seemed to think there was anything strange about her being hired, and Erica breathed a small sigh of relief. She would have hated any sexual innuendoes or smirks. They had to be curious, but they didn't push for explanations. Of course, it could be that Ryan had a habit of bringing home strange women. That thought didn't hold much appeal, either.

"I'll be out of commission for a few days, so I'll leave the work schedule to you, Zack. Just check in with me each evening until I'm back to full strength."

Erica finished her coffee while they spent a couple minutes talking ranch business. Then both men left as quietly as they'd entered.

Remembering that cooking was supposed to be part of her new duties, she asked Ryan what he wanted to eat and then managed to make them some toast without burning it. When they'd finished, he walked her through the house, which was divided by a wide hallway that linked the kitchen with the front foyer. He showed her all the formal rooms first. They were beautifully decorated with expensive furnishings and looked picture-perfect, but unused.

On the opposite side of the hallway there was a family room that looked comfortable and lived-in. Furnished in shades of brown, copper and blues, it had a TV, a large leather sofa and recliners. Off the family room was the ranch office where Ryan had spent the night.

"This is where I spend most of my time," he told her. "When I'm not outside, I'm keeping up with the business end of the ranch. The records need work right now because there's been so much else to do. I'm hoping you can help me get caught up."

Erica just nodded. She didn't know much about the ranching industry, but she had enough business training and experience to cope with any basic operation. Just being near the high tech equipment gave her an incredible sense of security. Her fingers actually itched to feel a keyboard.

Ryan leaned against the edge of the desk, crossed his arms over his chest, and stared at her. "You have the look of an addict in withdrawal, lusting after my computer."

Erica snapped her gaze back to his. "I do not. I'm just naturally curious," she argued. In fact, what she really lusted after was her cell phone. She'd left it in the glove box of her car so that she wouldn't be tempted to call home.

Another thought occurred to her. "Do you have an Internet connection?" There was no disguising her excitement.

"I have a modem and ISP, but service is erratic out here."

"You don't have unlimited access?"

"More like, pay by the minute at long-distance rates."

"Ouch," she said, scrunching her nose. "I guess Internet surfing isn't that practical then, is it?"

"Nope. Do you have an email account back home in Philly?"

"Chicago," Erica corrected, then bit her lip. She glared at Ryan, annoyed that he'd wormed that information out of her.

His grin was wickedly challenging. "Chicago, huh? Is it just a step on the corporate ladder or is it really your home?"

"What makes you think I'm the corporate type?"

"You have 'upwardly mobile' written all over you. That's why I'm so curious as to why you've been tending bar at Bubba's."

A frown creased her brow. "What makes the difference?"

"Just naturally inquisitive," he teased.

She changed the subject. "Is this the end of the tour?"

"You slept in my room last night." He pointed to the opposite door. "That leads to the laundry room, a half-bath and back to the kitchen."

"How many rooms upstairs?"

"A master suite, a couple guest suites and a room that the owner's son uses occasionally. The third floor is the old servants' quarters but it's mostly used for storage."

"Who owns this place?"

"What difference does it make?"

Erica flashed him another look of annoyance, but didn't force the issue. It really didn't matter if he told her or not. The fewer people she encountered, the better.

"A pretty big place for just one person."

"Yeah," he agreed, "the owners bought it as an investment, but they don't care much for country life."

"This is an investment property and you're a live-in manager?"

He frowned. "Something like that." Suddenly impatient with the conversation, he took Erica's arm and ushered her back to the main hallway. A wide, spiraling staircase led to the upper floor.

"You can take your pick of the rooms upstairs. I'll show you around up there if you want."

"That's not necessary," she said, gently withdrawing from his touch. It amazed her that such an impersonal gesture could send a shiver of excitement over her body. "I know you don't feel like running up and down stairs, and I'm sure I can find my way."

She'd only taken one step up the stairs when he tugged her to a halt by grasping the back of her sweatshirt. Erica turned and found herself almost nose to nose with him.

Kept at arm's length he was a threat to her composure. Up close, he stirred a response she didn't want to acknowledge. Her pulse picked up rhythm, dancing a jig against her skin.

"Yes?" She tried to infuse the right amount of disinterest in her tone so he wouldn't realize how much his proximity unnerved her. "You need something?"

"Not right away, but I would like some help with my shower after you get settled."

Erica's imagination abruptly conjured images of naked bodies glistening with moisture. They were sensuously steamy, wildly exciting and way too disturbing for her peace of mind. Her heart skittered recklessly until she reined it in.

Propping hands on her hips, she battled her own jumbled emotions with righteous indignation. "If you think helping you bathe is part of my job description, then you've got another think coming. We either keep it strictly business between us or I'm outta here," she threatened.

Ryan lifted one brow as if to question her sanity. "All I need is help covering my cast with plastic. Doc said to tie a bag around it when I shower, and I can't do it one-handed."

Erica felt heat creeping up her cheeks. Embarrassed for overreacting to his simple request, she was at a loss at how to save face. Deciding that a hasty retreat was in order, she turned and dashed up the stairs, calling to him over her shoulder. "Give me fifteen minutes."

* * * * *

Ryan grinned. The lady had spunk, but her sassy scolding didn't dampen his interest. The fierce chemistry between them had her rattled, and he liked that. He liked it a lot.

Innocent blushes were probably far from the norm for a sophisticated city girl. He'd be willing to bet his favorite horse that not many people saw Erica Smyth blush.

It had been a long time since he'd been so keenly interested in a woman. A long time since he'd felt the hungry stir of excitement that was more than just a physical itch. The lady might not have plans to stay long, but that didn't mean they couldn't enjoy getting to know each other before she left.

He watched until her shapely tush disappeared from sight and headed to his bedroom, pulling his shirt from the waistband of his jeans. Then he tried to jerk the shirt over his head and sucked in a harsh breath as pain shot through his ribs.

Moving more carefully, he tugged the shirt past the cast and tossed it aside. His movements were slow and awkward, but he'd have to get used to it for a while. After kicking off each boot, he eased himself onto the bed and took a deep, cautious breath. His arm and ribs were throbbing, his face felt stiff and swollen, and nearly every inch of his body ached.

All he wanted was a few minutes' rest, but as soon as he closed his eyes the phone rang, jarring him to attention again. He swore softly and reached for the receiver. "Havens."

"It's about time you answered your damned phone."

Sighing, Ryan relaxed again. He wasn't in the mood to deal with an irascible bar owner, but he needed the issue settled.

"Bubba."

"You owe me ten thousand for the brawl you started."

Ryan snorted. "You've never had more than a thousand dollars worth of furniture in the place, and you know it."

"I won't take a penny less than five, or we go to court."

"Fine by me. Send a bill, and I'll pay any reasonable charges. Try to gouge me, and I'll sue you and the Turleys for damages. Win or lose, it's going to cost you to collect."

There was a long pause while Bubba mulled over his choices. "I'll take three thousand."

"Send me an itemized bill, and I'll cut a check as soon as you pay Erica the week's wages you owe her."

Bubba responded with a spate of vulgarities. They argued a little longer, then he tried to weasel out with the excuse that she hadn't left a forwarding address.

"She works for me now. Send her money with the bill. Cash, and don't try to stiff her or I'll take it from your payment."

With that, Ryan hung up and sagged against the pillows. He closed his eyes, wanting nothing more than quiet and stillness.

* * * * *

Fifteen minutes later, Erica hesitantly entered his shadowy room through the door he'd left ajar. Although the color scheme of Ryan's bedroom was a startling passion red and black, the rest was typically masculine with heavy furniture and no-frills decor.

Tiptoeing closer to the bed, she watched the even rise and fall of Ryan's bare chest. His slow, steady breathing convinced her that he was sleeping soundly, and she didn't want to disturb him. He needed rest more than a shower.

Feeling somewhat of a voyeur, she couldn't resist studying him as he slept. His chest and shoulders were tanned, broad and muscled. His nipples were tantalizing dark spots tucked amidst fine, golden curls. Except for some darkening bruises, his torso was every bit as gorgeous as the rest of him.

Her gaze drifted along the arrow of hair on his flat stomach to where it dipped beneath the denim of his jeans. The worn, faded fabric stretched over the sexy bulge that proclaimed him male and hugged thighs that she'd learned firsthand were hard and strong.

Heat invaded her cheeks again, but this time it had nothing to do with embarrassment. The feeling didn't stop with her face, either. It washed over her whole body, making her shudder with a reaction too involuntary to explain.

She wanted to slide right into bed with him and press her body against his, to feel again the wild surge of excitement she'd felt last night when they'd kissed. The urge was so strong she shuddered and abruptly turned to leave the room.

Physical desire had never been a big issue for her. She'd been attracted to lots of men without becoming obsessed with their bodies. None of them had ever sparked such a volatile response in her. Ryan was rapidly becoming irresistible, and therefore a decided threat to her carefully laid plans.

Deciding to familiarize herself with her temporary home while he slept, Erica left his room. She glanced at his computer as she moved through the office, but didn't want to use it without asking first. Booting up someone's personal computer without permission was like peeking into his or her underwear drawer. It just wasn't right.

The bath and utility rooms were small, but neat and clean. She wondered if Ryan was tidy or if he hired a cleaning staff. Was cleaning and laundry part of a housekeeper's job description? It hadn't occurred to her to ask, but she supposed it might be.

Dottie, her parents' housekeeper, supervised the cleaning staff, but didn't actually do the cleaning. She cooked and took care of laundry, so maybe that's what Ryan expected. Or maybe he expected her to do it all while nursing him back to health.

The idea made her frown, but it was quickly replaced by a smile as she entered the kitchen. It was filled with gleaming, modern appliances that looked easy enough to use. She wasn't as inept a cook as she'd lead him to believe, but neither was she a gourmet. She'd just never spent much time cooking.

The family business had always been more important to her. The corporate world was the center of her universe. She loved pitting her mental strength against some of the world's top executives. She thrived on the challenges of investment strategies, of keeping their company on the cutting edge of technology, and of acquiring newer and bigger accounts.

All that aside, she had to worry about her temporary job first. Ryan's cupboards and refrigerator were well stocked. If she was to be in charge of meals, they'd have to be simple, so she needed a plan.

Chapter Four

"If you don't hold still, I'm going to slit your throat," Erica warned menacingly.

They'd spent three solid days cooped up in the house because of steady rain. Fighting the attraction between Ryan and her had been an endless, exhausting battle—one they were no closer to winning. Both of them were beyond irritable.

"I'd hold still if you'd quit rubbing up against me like a damn cat," he grumbled.

Erica clenched her teeth and stepped away from him, deciding to count to ten. She only made it to five.

"I can't very well shave you and stay out of reach, now can I? Why don't you just let your stupid beard grow?"

"It itches like hell," he complained, shifting restlessly in the straight-back kitchen chair.

"Do you want to try doing it with your left hand?"

"I'll slice my face to shreds."

Erica took a deep breath. She'd been doing a lot of that to try and calm herself. It didn't work, but she took pride in trying. "In that case, cowboy, you just have to put up with having me close."

Ryan heaved a tormented sigh and closed his eyes. "Then try not to rub your breasts against me. I have a thing for breasts."

Her mouth dropped open and she took another step back, hardly believing her ears. It was the first personal remark he'd made during their enforced captivity, and it was a lulu.

When she didn't say anything to break the stunned silence, he opened his eyes and pinned her with an unrepentant gaze.

"You have a thing?" she finally choked out.

"Yeah," he drawled, holding her gaze with his beautifully hypnotic eyes. "A thing. I'm especially partial to that part of a woman's anatomy."

Erica thought she might hyperventilate. She forced herself to breathe deeply again. She didn't want to know about his fetish. Her breasts had always been sensitive to the lightest touch.

"My arms are attached to the rest of my torso," she enunciated each word slowly and carefully. "And since my arms aren't six feet long, I can't shave you unless I have my whole torso close to you."

"I understand that," he said, speaking as slowly and politely as she, "but having your breasts pressed against me is damn arousing."

"Arousing?" She nearly choked on the word. "I'm not doing anything even remotely seductive."

"You're breathing, aren't you?" he argued, his gaze dropping to the rise and fall of her chest.

The intensity of his regard made her nipples tingle and tighten. They grew plump, pressing against the fabric of her bra and T-shirt. The reaction brought a gleam of satisfaction to his eyes, and she lost her temper.

"That's it!" She threw up her hands in frustration. "I'm not helping you any more. Slice your face to ribbons or let it itch like hell. I don't care! I am wiping my hands of this whole process!"

When she started to turn from him, he grasped her arm with his good hand, holding her firmly. She glared at him even as his touch sent a jolt of electricity zinging up her arm.

"If you don't let go of me this very second, your good arm is going to be useless, too," she warned darkly.

Ryan loosened his grip, but didn't completely release her. "How could I forget? You're a black belt in karate, right? You could probably snap my bones like toothpicks, couldn't you?"

His voice softened into a soothing, coaxing tone. His thumb was gently rubbing the pulse at her wrist. "If I apologize nicely, will you finish my shave?"

Erica continued to glare at him. He was completely shameless. She wondered if he'd spent his whole life manipulating women until they gave him what he wanted.

"I guess that depends on the apology." She tugged her hand from his grasp, not quite ready to forgive him.

He expelled an exaggerated sigh. "I'm deeply sorry if I've said or done anything to inflame you."

She drew back an arm as if to smack him.

He held up a hand in protest. "Okay, okay. I'm sorry, and I really need your help."

Erica relaxed a bit. "That's a pretty pathetic apology."

"Cut me a little slack here, honey. I'm not used to being incapacitated, and I'm not very experienced in the apology department, either."

"Don't call me honey. It's nothing but bee dung, and I'm not the least bit impressed with your sweet talk."

Ryan sighed again. "You're a hard woman, Erica Smyth."

"Yeah, well, I'm the only one here at the minute, if you need reminding. So we'll do things my way." She stepped close again and picked up the razor. "Spread your legs."

He feigned shock at her command, but shifted his legs so she could step between them. His shaving cream-lathered mouth tilted in a rakish grin, lightening the tension between them.

"The barber never stands between my legs."

She used one hand to tilt his head and began the shaving process again. "The barber has one of those fancy swivel chairs, a lot more experience than I do, and probably longer arms."

"But no breasts," he mumbled.

In the process of dragging the safety razor down his cheek, she halted infinitesimally and gave him a low warning growl. "Keep your mouth shut."

"Okay, okay." His words were only a hiss of air.

Erica took several slow swipes with the razor. Then she turned to rinse the blades in a bowl of water and repeated the process. For the next few minutes, the silence was only broken by the sound of their breathing. Ryan's face was no longer swollen and the cuts were healed. All that was left of the bruising was a little discoloration. Still, her actions were slow and careful.

After shaving the larger, easier areas of his cheeks, she moved to the more difficult angles of his jaw, chin and neck. Her tongue slid across her lips as though to guide the razor.

While Erica concentrated on the job at hand, Ryan tried to concentrate on anything and everything but the involuntary movement of her tongue and the lush breasts so near his face.

The last three days had been rough. He'd slept a lot, but had spent nearly every waking minute with his sexy houseguest. Every tick of the clock had them squaring off in some fashion.

She cooked food that was too hard for him to chew with a swollen jaw. She couldn't cook anything that needed more than one ingredient, and she had a tendency to burn that lone ingredient.

He'd had to teach her how to use the dishwasher. She hadn't known how to use the washer and dryer, either, or how to sort the clothes. As a domestic technologist she was sadly lacking in skills. She hadn't even known how to switch on the vacuum cleaner.

There was no doubting her grit, though. Regardless of how frustrated she became with a task, she kept trying. Never satisfied with just doing something right, she wanted to excel at everything.

Right now his lovely barber was excelling at battering his self-control. His gaze stayed glued to her mouth as she sucked on her tongue, and he badly wanted to do the same.

Despite her annoyance with him, she was very gentle. The slow, steady caress of each stroke had inadvertently stroked a fire in his loins. Everything this woman did made him hot. He'd thought their forced proximity might dull his interest, but it had only intensified. She continued to challenge him both physically and intellectually. Her quick wit and wicked sense of humor seemed a perfect complement to his.

He knew they should ignore the wild sexual attraction they shared, but his body was way past the point of pretending. The slow, steady throb that once pulsed in his broken hand had somehow shifted below his belt. Now he had a whole new ache to contend with, and not much hope of relief.

"I think that's all," Erica commented as she set aside the razor. She picked up a washcloth and wiped shaving foam from his cheeks. Then, using the towel draped around his neck, she slowly patted the excess moisture from his face.

As she leaned back a little to study her handiwork, Ryan shifted his legs to hold her captive between his thighs. Their gazes locked. Hers held silent reprimand, his a challenge so bold that it sucked the air from her lungs.

She could have resisted the challenge. He'd been challenging her on one level or another since the instant they'd met. She'd gotten good at volleying his challenges. What caught her off guard this time was the sudden, unexpected flare of need in his beautiful eyes; a primitive flash of hunger that staggered her breathing and sent a shudder of matching desire through her.

"Ryan?" She couldn't get more than a whisper past the tightness of her throat, and she knew her eyes were mirroring the need she saw in his.

"What?" he asked. His gaze never wavered from hers, but his thighs tightened to pull her closer. The heat of his touch branded her flesh as he brought both hands to rest on her hips.

Deciding, just this once, to throw caution to the wind, she dropped both her hands to his broad shoulders. She'd been aching to caress the smooth, firm flesh. There was no sense denying it any longer. For three days now he'd been wearing nothing but sweatpants, enticing her with an overload of gorgeous, naked flesh.

She wanted to explore the hard, sinewy muscles and bronzed skin that had delighted her eyes and teased her senses. She wanted to know the feel of his flesh against her own. The need was as fierce as it was foreign.

"We shouldn't start something we might not be able to control," she whispered, running her fingers lightly over his chest, gently raking her nails through the wiry golden curls.

"Who says losing control is such a bad thing?"

"Me," she managed before her breathing grew shallower. His good hand cupped her right breast, squeezing gently and making it swell with need. He used the fingers of his other hand to tickle the nipple of her left breast.

Her legs trembled. Someone moaned softly, and Erica was pretty sure the sound originated in her throat. "I'm a control freak, remember?" Her eyes pleaded with him to understand her reservations and vulnerability.

All their tentative exploration was done in slow motion with each being careful not to move too fast, not to do anything that might alarm the other, nor unleash a torrent of passion.

He shifted, sliding a leg between her thighs and urging her to straddle his lap. When she nestled closer, the feel of his thick, hard arousal sent a shaft of liquid fire to the center of her body. She instinctively arched into his hardness.

It was his turn to groan. His eyelids dropped, shielding his reaction from her watchful gaze. She didn't want him hiding his emotions, so she ground herself against him harder. Cupping his face in her hands, she dropped her mouth to his.

"There's no harm in losing control once in a while," he murmured against her lips.

"Shut up and kiss me," she whispered back.

Ryan didn't need to be asked twice. He took her mouth with greedy hunger, thrusting his tongue into the warm, sweet depths and doing his own exploring. Their tongues dueled, dancing in sinuous pleasure, and then he sucked hers deeply into his mouth.

He tilted his head, angled their lips closer so that he could have even more of her. She tasted every bit as delicious as he remembered. He strained to get his fill, but he'd been wanting too long to be easily appeased.

When his lungs started to burn, he lifted his mouth just long enough for both of them to draw air. Then he captured her lips again, plunging his tongue back into her honeyed warmth.

Erica's arms were locked around his neck. He kept his cast across her back, but slid the fingers of his other hand into the wild tangle of her hair. He'd wanted to know the feel of it since the first time he'd seen her. It was thick and soft with springy curls that coiled around his fingers. He loved the weight and texture of it. Pressing a handful tightly against her nape, he tugged her head closer.

She was wearing sweat pants and a T-shirt. Ryan was wearing less, but every layer of fabric between them was one too many. He bucked his hips, rubbing against the heated cradle of her thighs, frustrated by all the constrictive clothing.

Finally dragging his mouth from hers, he pleaded huskily, "Help me." Then he was tugging at the hem of her shirt.

A touch of wariness entered her eyes. He tried to control his impatience, tried to smile and reassure her. "Please?" he coaxed. "I want to see you."

She hesitated another instant, and then rewarded him with a trusting, heart-stopping smile. "The breast thing?"

His throat closed on any reply. His blood was pounding so loudly in his ears that he could hardly hear, yet the teasing lilt of her voice echoed straight to his heart. He held her gaze, returned her smile and nodded his agreement.

She pulled the shirt over her head and tossed it aside. Ryan drew in another ragged breath. The pulse throbbing at her throat beckoned his mouth, so he placed a kiss there first. Her skin was soft and sweet. It smelled of flowers and woman. He inhaled deeply, locking the scent into his memory.

He had to stroke her long, elegant neck with his tongue. As with everything else about her, her taste was unique and fascinating. Her flesh was warm and smooth and impossibly soft.

Ryan had to rein in his control before allowing his caresses to progress to the roundness of her breasts. His breathing grew more ragged as he lifted his gaze to hers again.

"I want more."

Erica held his gaze as she very slowly reached behind her back and unclipped her bra. She hesitated and brought her hands back to her sides, unresisting, yet not totally baring herself.

"Don't be shy," he begged, nibbling at her lips until she clutched his head and deepened the kiss. They shared another hot, sweet kiss that had them swallowing each other's moans.

Ryan dragged his mouth from hers and planted a row of kisses down her throat to the curve of her shoulder. He nudged the bra strap off and followed the soft swell of her breast until he was close enough to tease a nipple with his tongue.

He felt Erica's body clench around him, arms and legs tightening along with her nipple. Her chest began to heave with each breath, pressing the plump fullness of her breast against his mouth as he continued to suckle. The nipple swelled against his tongue, making his body swell with explosive need.

Her fingers were clenching and unclenching his hair like a cat flexing its claws. She undulated against him, increasing the pressure of her feminine demands. Desire clawed at his gut, too, but he refused to be rushed.

He'd been starving for her, craving a chance to touch, taste and feel. He wanted to savor every second of this closeness. As he lifted his mouth from the hard, wet nipple, he moved it to the other, caressing with his lips and tongue.

Erica was writhing against him impatiently now, making urgent little sounds that coaxed without words. He wanted to see and feel more of her, every inch. He wanted her out of her pants, yet he didn't want to shift her far enough away to accomplish the goal.

Instead, he lifted his head for another kiss. When their mouths locked he pulled her hard against his chest, rubbing her taut nipples against his equally tight ones.

Keeping his casted arm behind her back, Ryan slid his left hand beneath the waistband of her pants. Erica stiffened slightly as he stroked the soft skin of her waist. She dug her fingers into his shoulders as he slid his hand to her stomach.

"Ryan!"

He halted his exploration at her protest. Looking into her eyes again, he saw wariness warring with passionate need.

"Trust me," he begged against her lips as their jagged breaths mingled with another kiss. "Let me love you."

When her body relaxed again, he took it as a sign of faith. Then his mouth drifted back down to a taut nipple. He sucked greedily and shuddered as her fingernails sunk into his shoulders.

It grew harder to concentrate once her touch began to stray. Her fingers drifted to his chest as she focused on exploring him. Her touch was soft, but sure, shy, yet needy. His heart raced, his body throbbed and his ears were ringing.

He stilled Erica's hands with his good one, drawing in a rasping breath and fighting for control. Bells kept ringing in his ears. Their passion-hazed gazes locked as they simultaneously realized the bells they heard were door chimes.

Ryan mumbled a string of oaths while struggling to catch his breath. He coaxed Erica to ignore the summons. "They'll go away eventually," he insisted, trying to keep a grip on her as she slid off his lap.

"What if it's important?"

His frustration mounted as she turned her back to him and pulled on her bra and shirt. "I'm not expecting anyone, and if I go to the door now, I'm going to kill whoever it is anyway."

She turned back to him. His snarling threat amused her. He could tell from the sudden twinkle in her eyes. He grudgingly returned the smile and felt some of his own tension easing.

"I imagine it's another of your neighbors," she offered.

His city girl probably wasn't used to guests showing up uninvited and unannounced, but things were a lot different in these parts. Over the past couple days, several of his neighbors had stopped by to bring food and see if he needed anything.

"Everybody in the county knows you're confined to the house because of the weather," she added. "If we don't answer the door, whoever it is will go to the barns searching. Then we'll have the whole staff to deal with."

The bell rang again. "Just answer it and pretend you've been resting. I'll stay out of sight."

Ryan rose from the chair, tugged at his sweatpants a little and headed toward the front of the house, grumbling all the way. He pulled open the door just as his guest was heading back down the walk. She turned, and he relaxed.

"Trudy, it's good to see you. Sorry it took me so long." He stepped out the door onto the porch.

Trudy Sanders was an attractive woman in her late fifties. She owned the best restaurant in town. He would never intentionally hurt her feelings, so he returned her warm smile and affectionate hug.

"Ryan, it's good to see you, too, but I'm sorry if I woke you," she apologized. "I've just been so crazy busy that this is the first free minute I've had to come and see you."

"Don't worry about it," he said, happy that she attributed his tangled hair and heated skin to sleep. "I know the restaurant gets busier when it rains. Everybody who can't work is eating."

She laughed. "That's about the size of it, and I've been swamped. So how are you getting along? Is your arm bothering you much?"

"Nah, the worst of the soreness is gone already. It's just a hairline crack and shouldn't take long to heal."

"Meantime, you have to do everything left-handed, right?"

"Yes, ma'am. I'm not likin' it much, but I'm learnin'."

"What about help? Do you have anyone to help around the house with cooking and chores?"

"Yes, ma'am. I hired someone to help for a couple weeks."

"Well, I'm glad. You're always the first to help anyone else in need, so you shouldn't hesitate to ask for help."

"Thanks, Trudy, I appreciate that."

"Speaking of which," she said, turning toward the porch steps. "I almost forgot why I came. I have a car full of food for you. I cooked a few of your favorites and put them in containers. You can refrigerate some and freeze the rest."

Ryan followed her, listening to her chatter as he drew in a deep breath of the rain-drenched evening air. It felt good to be outdoors. The sky was clearing and the forecast for the rest of the week was good. Things could get back to normal.

"You'd better let me carry everything," suggested Trudy. "I can make a couple trips if you'll get the doors."

He didn't argue, just held out both his arms. "This cast comes in handy once in a while," he teased, encouraging her to stack the Styrofoam trays on them.

They had their arms full as they approached the house again, and Ryan called to Erica. She was at the door within a minute and opened it for them. He made quick introductions as they all headed down the hallway to the kitchen.

"Trudy Sanders, Erica Smyth."

"Nice to meet you," they chorused in unison, then smiled.

Erica had pulled her hair into a demure knot at her nape. The wild flush had left her cheeks, and she looked her prim and proper self again. Ryan heaved a silent sigh of regret.

"I can't tell you how glad I am that Ryan has someone here to help," said Trudy. "Spring is such a busy time for ranch folks and everyone feels guilty for not pitching in and helping him more. He's usually the one doing so much for his neighbors and friends. We hate not to be able to return the many favors."

Her praise made him shift uncomfortably. "Nobody owes me any favors, and I have a whole staff taking care of the work."

"Several people have called and stopped by," said Erica. "And there are always ranch employees in shouting distance."

"It's still a big relief to know that you're here, dear. I slipped on some ice a few years back and broke my wrist. I couldn't even cut my own meat. It was such a darned nuisance."

"I'll second that," he said. "I'm not very good with my left hand, so even the small stuff can be aggravating."

Trudy nodded her understanding, and then supervised the storage of more than a dozen large containers of food. "I've marked everything so you'll know what's inside," she explained. "Katlyn made a cheesecake for you. Just so your sweet tooth won't suffer."

"Katlyn's your daughter?" asked Erica.

Ryan shot her a frown.

"She's my niece," said Trudy, "Have you met her?"

"No, but I overheard someone mention a blessed event."

Trudy beamed, and Ryan's frown deepened. He searched Erica's face while Trudy extolled Katlyn's virtues and raved about her great-nephew. Erica politely grilled the other woman, but her expression didn't offer a hint at what she was feeling.

He tried to remember if any of his other visitors had mentioned Katlyn, but he didn't think so. How had Erica learned about her, and what did she know?

Chapter Five

"Trudy brought some salad, lasagna and garlic bread. How's that sound for dinner? Think you can chew everything?"

After bidding their guest goodbye, they'd gone back to the kitchen. "My jaw's fine now. It doesn't hurt to chew, and Trudy makes some of the best lasagna I've ever eaten."

"That's settled then. Sit down, and I'll get the food on the table. It'll only take a couple minutes."

Ryan didn't like having her wait on him any more than necessary, so he collected some glasses and silverware. He could set the table one-handed even if he was slow about it.

They worked in silence while an inexplicable tension mounted between them. He noticed she was very careful not to brush up against him. The fact that she was deliberately avoiding his touch irritated the hell out of him.

Was she uptight about their earlier loving? For giving in to the sizzling desire between them? Was she regretting a loss of control? Lamenting their lapse into pure sensual pleasure?

Or was it Trudy's mention of Katlyn that had caused her to get so tense and quiet? He didn't know how she could have any knowledge of the other woman's importance to him. Besides, Katlyn was married with a child now. Totally off-limits.

The uncomfortable silence continued while they ate. Ryan didn't know what to say, so he didn't prod her with questions. He figured he'd have to wait for the answers and hope their budding relationship hadn't taken two steps backward.

"You're right," she said when she'd finished her portion of the meal. "Everything was delicious."

He hoped the good food would improve her mood, but he wisely refrained from commenting on it. He'd eaten twice as much as her and was feeling stuffed, but content.

"Would you like some of that cheesecake?"

"I'd better wait a while for dessert. I already ate my fill. You go ahead and have some if you want."

"Maybe later," she said, starting to rise from her seat.

"Sit still a minute," he suggested softly. He searched her eyes for a hint of what was bothering her, but her expression was guarded. "What's the rush? It's not like either of us has anywhere to go this evening."

Erica eased back into her chair and he tried to lighten the tension by teasing. "Don't tell me you're in a hurry to escape my charming company."

"Which grows less charming with each additional day of confinement," she noted.

Her sassy response pleased him, and he grinned unabashedly. "I never could stand being cooped up indoors for long. Now that my hand's stopped aching and the rain seems to be over for a while, I'll be able to get back to work."

"What about the ribs? You're still not moving too fast."

"They'll be better in the morning, too."

"Doc said to give your arm a couple weeks before you get active again."

"He just said two weeks so that I'd give it a few days."

"Is that right?" she taunted, eyes glinting with the light of challenge. "It's some sort of special cowboy interpretation of the doctor's diagnosis?"

"Sure," he drawled, holding her gaze and flirting for all he was worth. "Every cowboy knows the special healing rules. Regular guys, two weeks; cowboys, two days."

"You're all so tough, huh? At that rate, you should be able to come out of that cast in about three more days."

"Damn, I'd like that," he said on a sigh. "Suppose I could convince Doc to cut it off early?"

"Probably, if you sign a waiver releasing him of all responsibility for your stupidity."

Ryan flashed her another grin. "You're a hard-hearted woman, Red." She flinched at the nickname he'd chosen for her, but the reaction just made his grin widen. "Not an ounce of compassion."

"I have plenty of compassion. I just don't waste it on guys who pick fights with men twice their size."

It was the first time she'd mentioned the fight all day. He'd been hoping the subject was dead and wondered what had prompted her to scold now.

"Not even if it's on your behalf?"

"Was it on my behalf?" she asked, her tone thoughtful. "I don't think we ever established just why you felt like fighting Saturday night."

Dangerous territory. Ryan didn't want to go there, but he could tell by the determined glint in her eyes that she wasn't going to drop the subject. "I might have been a little tired, irritable and under the influence," he suggested.

She gave him a long, measuring look that made him feel about five years old and antsy enough to squirm in his seat.

"Just having a bad night?"

A bad night, bad week, bad year, he thought grimly. One of the longest and most frustrating of his life. In the space of ten months, the only woman he'd ever loved had met, married and borne the child of another man.

The reminder dampened his mood. "Everybody has 'em."

"Just thinking of her depresses you, doesn't it? Why deny it? You got in a fight because you were nursing a bruised ego, and it's nobody's fault but your own that you got hurt." That said, she rose from the table and started cleaning the kitchen.

"It has nothing to do with ego," he declared flatly.

"No? Then exactly what does it have to do with? A romance gone wrong? A broken heart? Were you and Katlyn an item before she married someone else? Did she jilt you at the altar?"

"Nothing like that," he snapped, his jaw tight.

"Nothing personal or emotional?" she prodded. "That's why you felt like smashing people and furniture?"

"She's my best friend."

"Friends and lovers?" she asked softly, pinning him with curious, watchful eyes.

"She's not that type of woman."

As soon as the words were said, Ryan saw Erica stiffen, and knew he'd just stuck his foot in his mouth.

"What type of woman would that be?" she asked. "The type of woman who works in bars? Who picks up strange men?"

He'd learned that she had a temper to go with her red hair. It became more obvious with each successive question.

"Is Katlyn the type who's beyond temptation? Who'd never consider engaging in premarital sex? One of those nice girls who thinks physical satisfaction is wicked outside of marriage?"

He clenched his jaw. "That's not what I meant. She's not a prude, and I'm not a hypocrite. Her feelings for me were strictly platonic. We were never lovers."

He held his breath as Erica stared directly into his eyes, her gaze searching. His explanation soothed her ruffled feathers a bit, but her next question hit a little too close for comfort.

"Not through any choice of yours, I take it?"

He flinched at the accuracy of her taunt, and decided it was time to halt the discussion. "Are you ready to exchange secrets, Red? Ready to confess all your deepest, darkest emotions? Or are you just interested in probing mine?"

She surprised him with a cheeky grin. "I thought it was worth a try," she said. "You're not very forthcoming with personal information even though you're good at prying."

"Trying to pry," he countered, relaxing a little. "You're not very good at sharing personal information, either. I still don't know any more about you than I did on Saturday."

"That's not completely true," she argued.

He conceded the point. "I know you're an inept housekeeper and an expert at arguing."

She scrunched her nose at him. "I'm not inept, just untutored, and I only argue when you're wrong, like now. You've learned a lot about me—all my favorite authors, movies and television shows. Entertainment seems to be the one subject we've analyzed to death."

"Not much else to do on rainy days. Not that you were willing to do, anyway," he added with wicked amusement. "But I've also learned that you're an upwardly mobile executive from Chicago, that you have a nasty temper and an incredible body."

His teasing brought a blush to her cheeks. He knew she hated the telltale reaction, but he was getting real fond of it.

He'd also stoked an emerald fire in her eyes, and she was really fabulous to watch when she was riled.

"I do not have a nasty temper," she insisted hotly. "You're just very good at provoking me. It must be a real talent for you judging by your track record."

"Track record?"

"The Turleys, remember? The bar fight you provoked that got us into this situation in the first place?"

"You just can't stop harping about that, can you? Bar fights aren't all that unusual in these parts, city girl."

"I don't imagine too many people tear up Bubba's place. He's a shark." Which brought to mind another topic. "I still can't believe you talked him into giving me my money."

Bubba had shown up bright and early Monday morning with a bill for damages. He'd grudgingly given Ryan the money he owed Erica. That hadn't satisfied her, she'd wanted details.

She'd wanted to know how bad his personal finances had been damaged, and he didn't want to discuss his finances with her. So far, she still believed he was a regular, working-class cowboy, and that suited him just fine. He'd spent most of his adult life dodging gold-digging women.

"Everybody involved in the fiasco should have paid, not just you," she insisted. "You may have been itching for a fight, but you didn't throw the first punch, and you didn't smash anything."

Ryan didn't want to argue about it anymore. She was like a dog with a bone once she sunk her teeth into a subject.

"Let it go, Red."

She started to protest, then snapped her mouth shut and shook her head in resignation. Ryan just grinned at her. What he wanted was to pull her into his arms and pick up where they'd left off when Trudy interrupted them earlier. He didn't think luck was with him, though, so he didn't try.

He had an ache that just wouldn't quit where she was concerned. The last three days had been exhilarating as they'd learned to coexist, yet hadn't learned to trust each other enough to share anything more basic than personal entertainment preferences. Still, it was progress of a sort.

Erica busied herself clearing the table and loading the dishwasher. There wasn't much to do. Cleanup took less than five minutes. Then they were staring at one another again.

"What now?" she asked. "It's a little early for a movie."

"At least it's my turn to pick."

"It is not. We watched one of those kick-em-around, shoot-em-up and smash everything movies last night. It's my turn."

"It can't be. We've already watched every sad and sappy chick flick ever produced."

"We've barely touched the surface," she informed him airily. "Besides, you should be restricted from watching too much violence. You already exhibit a natural inclination toward violent behavior."

"The hell."

"See, you even pick up bad language from those wicked films."

"I know a whole helluva lot about romance, too, if you want another sample of my skills in that department."

Their gazes met and locked, fire flashing between them. A fierce rush of desire flared, but Erica swiftly smothered it.

"I'll pass," she said, turning her back to him again.

He could tell by the rigid set of her shoulders that she wasn't going to give the suggestion any consideration. He heaved a disgusted sigh. If sex was out, he'd have to find some other way to keep her close to him for the evening.

"If you ask real nice, we could go play with my computer," he finally suggested. He knew she'd been itching to check it out since her arrival, but he hadn't wanted her nosing into his files right away.

She turned and faced him. "Can we access the Internet?"

"If my server's working. We didn't have power outages with this last weather system, so it's probably okay."

Ryan slowly rose from his seat as he was talking. Sitting for even a brief spell made him stiff. The worst of the soreness was past, but there was still some tenderness.

He saw Erica's hand reach out to steady him, and then she snatched it back before making contact. He shot her a wry glance. "A little wary of the electric current between us?"

"I'm wary of you doing any more harm to yourself. I don't want a seriously injured invalid on my hands, even though I'm sure you'd get along fine without me."

He stepped aside so she could precede him to his office. "I'm not getting along just fine by myself. I have you, the ranch hands and a whole mess of helpful neighbors."

"You are really fortunate, you know. Some people would have to pay a very high price tag for the care you're getting."

"Hinting for a raise?"

"No." Her tone was firm. "I'm practically rolling in money since Bubba paid me, and I don't have to use it all for rent."

"What about at the end of your three weeks?" he probed. "Won't you need rent money when you go back to Chicago? Or do you have a roommate who takes care of the bills?"

"Roommate?" They'd reached his office. Erica stood aside while Ryan crossed the room and sat behind the desk.

"Roommate, lover, husband?"

She shook her head in exasperation. "You never stop prying. Why does it matter where I live when I go back?"

"I might have reason for concern if you have a jealous husband or ex-husband tucked away in the city," he said as he switched on the computer and monitor.

"I'm not married and never have been. Does that ease your mind?"

"Partly," he mumbled, feigning indifference. "Live-in lover?"

She sighed and moved around the desk. He shifted his chair out of the way and pulled a smaller one in front of the computer for her. She sat down and tossed him a rueful glance.

"When I go home, I'll live with my parents at no charge. Just like I've done for most my life."

"Except when you lived in a college dorm?"

"Yes, Sherlock. Purdue University to be exact."

"Business major?"

"Yes."

"So why are you here?"

"Leave of absence. Now stop with the interrogation and show me how to access the Internet."

* * * * *

He leaned closer, draping his left arm over the back of her chair. His warmth and scent engulfed Erica. The tangy spice of his shaving lotion had made an indelible mark on her senses. She'd never be able to smell it again without remembering the erotic thrill of sitting on his lap and sharing those long, heated kisses.

He always seemed to radiate heat as well, a warm, masculine heat that penetrated to a deep, secret part of her that had never been touched by any other man. The thought was unnerving.

"You have to use a dial-up for connection," said Ryan, showing her what icons to use and guiding her through the process. "Once you have an open connection to the Internet, just click on the icon and type in the address you want."

"Oh, this is the same program I use," she said with growing excitement.

She typed in her user name, ERICALSK.

"ERICALSK? What kind of name is that? I can see the Erica, but what's the rest stand for? Your initials?"

"Just gibberish." It was an abbreviated form of her full name, Erica Lynn Smyth-Kessler. He wasn't likely to recognize it, but she still didn't divulge it. "Close your eyes."

"Why?"

His tone was offended, but she didn't risk a glance at his expression. "So I can type in my password. You're never supposed to let anyone know your password."

"Tough."

Erica ignored him and tried to type so that he couldn't see which keys she used. She was immediately informed that she had mail and collected a list of more than fifty messages.

Ryan whistled softly. "That's quite a pile of emails."

"I haven't checked it for three weeks."

"I don't get that much in three months."

She skimmed through the listings, automatically deleting all the recognizable junk mail. She noticed a couple messages from her father and her cousin Steve, several from her friend, Beth, and the bulk from Geoffrey Wellman, the executive who got the promotion that should have been hers.

Geoffrey had been with the firm for a year, and the two of them had dated for a few months. She'd known her dad thought he was son-in-law material, but she hadn't known he thought Geoffrey was vice president material.

"Looks like KESEXEC is getting impatient for a response."

She noticed the same thing. The subject lines on Geoffrey's posts got more terse with each listing. She wanted to see what he had to say, but not with Ryan leaning over her shoulder.

Turning her head to ask him for some privacy, she was shocked to realize how close his face was to her own. His mouth was mere inches from hers. All thoughts of Geoffrey and her life back in Chicago vanished as her gaze mated with his.

Heat flared in his beautiful eyes and re-lit the fire that had churned within her earlier. She let her gaze roam the strong line of his jaw to the small cleft in his chin, studying each feature with an intensity born of an unaccustomed need.

His mouth was every bit as mesmerizing as his eyes. Now that she knew the feel of those full, firm lips, she found herself hungering for another taste of them.

"Such a wickedly pleasing mouth," she murmured, recalling the erotic pleasure his mouth had given her.

"Yours to command," he whispered as he inched closer.

Erica lifted a hand to cup the side of his face, stroking it with inquisitive fingers. His skin was warm and smooth, his jaw hard. She continued her slow, thorough scrutiny of his features as their bodies involuntarily swayed closer.

Ryan's left hand burrowed under her hair until she felt its warmth on her nape. Then he was tugging her close enough for their breaths to mingle and their mouths to meet.

Sweet, sweet pleasure. She was drowning in it, drawn under yet again by the seductive nibble at her lips and the slide of a hot tongue against her own. Time stood still and reality slipped away as she got lost in blissful, addictive sensations.

No other man's kisses had ever enthralled her like this, creating a raw need that threatened her composure and pulling her back again and again for the sweetness. No other kisses had ever tempted her beyond distraction. Never had she allowed a kiss to consume her the way this man's kiss was doing. It was new and fascinating and a little bit frightening.

"Ryan?" Erica barely recognized her own voice as their mouths parted and his name trembled on her lips.

"Tell me what you want." His voice was low and deep, like the rumble of distant thunder. "Anything."

"Everything, nothing, I don't know," she whispered in confusion. "It's too soon. We hardly know each other. There are too many reasons why we shouldn't give in to temptation. I want you, but I don't want to want you."

She'd never pleaded for anything in her life, but she needed time to come to terms with the powerful and unprecedented effect he had on her senses.

She wasn't promiscuous or wildly experienced with men. She didn't know how to handle this sudden, unexpected onslaught of primitive desire. She had a nagging, instinctive fear that making love with Ryan Havens could alter her life forever.

"Is that a request to back off?" he asked gruffly.

Erica searched his face, but she couldn't gauge his reaction to her stammered explanations. She didn't want to hurt him or have him think she was an uncaring tease. He had to know by her responses that she was wildly attracted to him.

"I need help controlling this thing between us."

She forgot to breathe for several long minutes while he studied her features as intently as she'd been studying his.

"Thing?" he finally asked with a touch of amusement.

He slipped his hand around her body and gently cupped her breast, brushing his thumb over her nipple in a butterfly caress. "Like the thing I have for breasts?"

Erica sucked in a breath, her whole body tightening. Her gaze never left the glittering intensity of his. "It's a powerful thing," she whispered with a catch in her voice.

He studied her features for a few more tension-filled minutes. "How about you help me get a bag on my arm, then I'll take a shower and let you read your email in private?"

Her breathing grew more irregular as he continued to hold her. Just being so close was enough to scatter her senses. She still wasn't sure what he expected.

"Take a shower as in 'slip into something more comfortable' or take a shower as in get ready for a good night's sleep?" she managed to ask.

A chuckle rumbled from his chest, and he gave her another quick hug before easing his chair backward.

"I mean complete reprieve," he teased. "You're always welcome to join me in bed, but I'm not some kind of predator. Making love isn't supposed to involve coercion."

Erica hated the telltale heat that stole up her neck. She'd always been susceptible to a blush, but she thought she'd outgrown the worst of her sensitivity. Not much embarrassed her. At least she hadn't thought so until she'd met him.

"That's my point," she argued quietly. "It wouldn't be making love at all. We aren't in love. We're just physically attracted to each other."

"That's where you're wrong, Ms. Smyth. People can make love without being in love. It happens all the time."

"That's just sex."

"No, it's not just about satisfying a bodily urge, it's about sharing yourself with someone you know and respect. It's about wanting to know each other in the most intimate fashion."

His words sent a quiver of desire coursing through Erica. She didn't want him to realize how much he tempted her, so she scoffed at him. "That sounds like a pretty smooth, well-rehearsed line to me."

Ryan threw back his head and laughed. Then he reached out his good hand to help her from her chair. "Come plasticate my arm so I can shower, and I'll leave you alone for a while."

She gently slipped from his grasp and led the way through his bedroom to his private bath.

"Plasticate? I don't think that's a real word."

He shook his head in resignation. "That's your problem. You think too much. You're always thinking too much and always arguing with me. You need to relax." He kept a collection of plastic grocery bags in the linen cupboard. She grabbed one, and then gently grasped his broken arm.

"Relax and learn to always agree with you? Become a little more pliable?" she challenged, slipping the bag over his cast, tying the ends and tucking them inside the plaster.

"Sounds like a plan to me."

She ignored him and checked her handiwork for possible leaks. "There," she pronounced him waterproof. "You're all plasticated. I'm going to go read my mail."

"I'll shower, and then pick a movie to watch later. Maybe something about outer space. That's pretty romantic, isn't it?"

She shook her head in resignation, finding pleasure in his wicked laughter. He really was an awful tease. He challenged her as no other man had ever done, mentally, physically and emotionally. Never in her wildest dreams had she imagined she could be attracted to a man on so many levels.

The steadily intensifying desire threatened all her preconceived ideas of who she was and what she wanted in life. Until Ryan, nothing had been more important to her than running her family's firm in the direction she wanted it to go.

She'd spent a lifetime training and striving tirelessly toward the top rung of the corporate ladder. Her life's goal hadn't suddenly changed, but what had seemed all-important a few days ago, seemed to be taking on less importance this week.

Last week she'd been nearly beside herself with impatience to return home and achieve that goal. This week, the impatience was being tempered by the charm of a handsome, blue-eyed devil.

Sitting back down at the computer, Erica slowly read and replied to her email. She assured her father and cousin that she was perfectly well and happy, promising to call home soon. She told her friend Beth that she was enjoying her vacation, and she told Geoffrey she would talk to him when she returned. She didn't offer any of them information as to where she was staying or what sort of job she was doing.

The men in her life had collectively insisted she couldn't exist without the company. They'd accused her of being totally dependent on the firm, both emotionally and economically. She intended to prove them wrong.

Sometimes you had to take a stand, she thought to herself. Actions spoke louder than words. Her absence was intended to make a statement, strong and clear. Either they gave her due respect or she'd leave Kesslers and strike out on her own.

She could and would leave the family business. She didn't want to, hated being forced to, but she would leave before compromising her personal and professional ethics.

Steve and Geoffrey had a different vision for the company and now Geoffrey was in a coveted position of power. His only concerns were dollars and cents, the corporate bottom line. Erica cared about the company's reputation, their clients and the employees who depended on them for their livelihood.

Her absence was proving, in no uncertain terms, that she was ready and able to back up her convictions with actions. At least, she hoped that's what it was proving. If they were doing fine without her, the plan could backfire. She'd known that from the onset. If they were taking advantage of her absence to proceed with major changes, then she'd already lost the battle.

Chapter Six

"I told you when I left that it might be a while before I got in touch," Erica said. She paced as far as the kitchen phone cord would allow while fielding her mother's questions.

"But three weeks? Didn't you realize we'd be concerned?"

Refined and dignified, Elaine Kessler never raised her voice above a soft, cultured timbre, but Erica could identify every tiny nuance. As soon as her mother had expressed relief at her call, her tone had filled with gentle reproof.

"What if you'd been in an accident?"

"Identification, Mother. You would have been informed."

"That's not the point."

"I'm on leave, vacation if you prefer. You've been telling me for years that I should relax and get away from work."

"But you're not vacationing. You're participating in some unnecessary power play with Geoffrey and your father. They said you swore you could get along without your wages. I shudder to think how you must be surviving."

Erica loved her mother dearly. She had a heart of gold and was intensely loyal, but she had no concept of how ordinary people lived. Born into money, she'd married into even more money and been pampered her entire life.

"I've never been afraid of work, Mother. I thrive on challenge. Why do you think I devote so much time to my career?"

"I know how hard you work, darling, but I also know you've always worked for your father. You can't be making much money, and I can't bear to think of you living in some hovel."

"I promise I have wonderful accommodations."

"You're staying with friends then?"

"No." Erica was sure her family had already been in touch with each of her friends in an effort to track down her whereabouts. It was time to change the subject.

"How's everything at Kesslers?"

Her mother's long-suffering sigh prompted a grin.

"Your father, Steven and Geoffrey have done nothing but fuss since you left. They're been absolute bears. The Turners refuse to negotiate with anyone but you, and Marge Peters told Geoffrey not to bother calling her at all until you get back."

Erica stopped pacing and stared out the window, her attention hundreds of miles away. "Steven arrogantly assured me he could handle the Turner account," she said, "and Geoffrey was just so positive he could charm Marge Peters. I know better. She has no patience with men. I warned Dad that their arrogance and chauvinism was getting out of control."

"Steven's still a bit immature," Elaine conceded.

"He's four years older than I am, Mother."

"Yes, darling, but you were born with more maturity. He's coming along, just slowly."

Erica gripped the receiver, her features tight with annoyance. "In the meantime, Dad's allowing him and Geoffrey to ignore my concerns and destroy the company. I won't have it."

"Well, if it's any consolation, I think they're getting the message. I can't say I approve of your methods, but I'm seeing results."

Whirling on her heel, Erica paced back across the kitchen, but halted abruptly when she caught sight of Ryan. Arms crossed over his chest, he was leaning against the doorframe, shamelessly eavesdropping on her private conversation.

Annoyed, she castigated him with angry eyes, even though her pulse skipped into overdrive at the sight of him. Dressed in snug, faded jeans and a navy T-shirt that hugged his chest and arms, he was totally buff.

Her mouth went dry. Every inch of him radiated blatant masculinity that tugged at everything feminine in her. The first sight of him each day still played havoc with her control. What was it about the man that made her feel so breathless and needy?

"Erica?" Her mother's demand for attention snapped her out of the sensual trance. She turned and lowered her voice.

"I'm sorry. I have to get back to work. I'll call again next week if you promise not to give this number to anyone."

"Of course, I promise, but your father's really worried."

Erica wasn't ready to go there.

"Love you. Bye." Ignoring her mother's protestations, she walked toward Ryan to hang up the phone. Then she crossed her arms over her chest to mimic his stance. Without voicing a word, she berated him.

He wasn't the least intimidated. His gaze fastened with hers while he taunted her with his newfound knowledge.

"So, there's a little power struggle in the family firm and you're having an extended temper tantrum, huh? Trying to force Daddy into seeing things your way?"

Erica saw red. She actually saw him through a haze of red—a direct result of having her blood boil, she was certain. For an instant she was too furious to speak. Damn the man for hitting so close to the truth, yet belittling the value of her efforts just like the rest of the men in her life.

"You have no idea what you're talking about, so don't insult me with your chauvinistic assumptions." She answered in a strained voice, battling to contain the anger shaking her whole body. "I'm fed up to the eyeballs with condescending males."

Ryan's brows slowly rose at her tone. He whistled, low and soft. "Direct hit, huh? So maybe you should fill me in on the details and set me straight."

"Why? It's none of your business."

"Humor me. I'm curious."

"And I should care?" she snapped as she continued to glare at him. At the moment, he epitomized everything that frustrated her about the male gender.

A brief silence fell between them as they continued the standoff. She watched his expression undergo a subtle change. His eyes slowly searched her features, making her wonder if he regretted his sarcastic remarks.

He seemed to give a little more thought to his next words. "If nothing else, I make a good sounding block. I've been told I have a head for business. Maybe I can help you work it out."

She doubted anyone could help, especially not someone who frequently made her lose sight of her goals. When she was with Ryan, she forgot the responsibilities that were so much a part of her normal life. He made her far too aware of feminine vulnerabilities.

Yet, his offer was probably as close to an apology as she would get. It wasn't his fault she was so furious with her dad, and she suddenly felt guilty for venting her anger on him.

The anger and tension drained from her as quickly as it had erupted. Turning toward the refrigerator, she said, "I was just going to start some breakfast. What would you like?"

"Bacon, eggs and an explanation," he said, moving further into the room and doing what he could to help set the table.

Erica mulled over what her mother had told her and realized she needed to talk about her situation. Having been absent from the corporate world these past few weeks, she felt disassociated and badly wanted an unbiased opinion.

"Microwave bacon and scrambled eggs okay?" she asked. She hadn't quite mastered the art of frying. At least, not without burning herself with grease and over or undercooking the eggs.

"Fine."

As she busied herself with food preparations, she slowly began to share some personal information.

"I've worked for my dad's firm since my teens. I've devoted my life to learning every aspect of the business. Since college, I've put in more time and effort than anyone on the payroll, and I finally earned an executive position last fall."

"You sound a little driven. Why? You obviously could have chosen any career path you wanted."

Erica shot him a glance. Few people understood her drive and determination, but she explained with all the passion she felt for her career choice.

"I chose corporate life because I love it. I've been fascinated with it since I was old enough to spend a day at the office with my dad. I never considered any other career.

"I love the daily challenges, the interaction with clients, and all the politics of putting together a million-dollar deal," she continued, the underlying excitement in her tone emphasizing her feelings. "I've always thrived on the fast pace, the wheeling and dealing, the highest level of decision-making and all the other aspects of the corporate world.

"I know it's hard for the average person to understand, but I guess I've got an overload of competitive genes. I need the challenge of pitting myself against some of the best minds in the business world. I don't just love it, I thrive on it."

The room went noticeably quiet after her impassioned speech. She slid a glance at Ryan. He'd finished setting the table and taken a seat. His expression had gone grim. She returned her attention to the food. A long, heavy silence fell as she cooked, then filled their plates. His expression was still tight when she plunked a plate in front of him.

"I suppose you're one of those men who think it's unwomanly to be so career-minded," she grumbled, her heart feeling strangely heavy at the thought.

When he didn't respond, she prompted, "Well?"

"Smells good," he said, still not looking at her.

Erica took her seat across from him and buttered her toast. "You have a problem with career-oriented women?"

Ryan finally lifted his head, letting his gaze lock with hers. "No, I don't have a problem with it, and no, I don't think it's unwomanly. I'm sure you're an exceptional executive and you have every right to be proud of what you do."

"Very tactfully put. So politically correct of you," she groused, stabbing her eggs with a fork, "maybe not too honest, but at least it's PC."

Some dark emotion flared in his eyes, but was quickly extinguished. "I don't lie, and I do believe in equal rights. I just don't share your passion for the corporate jungle."

"You understand it, but don't share it?" She wanted him to clarify his feelings.

"Oh yeah," he grimaced, attacking his food with more force than necessary, "I understand it well enough. I just tend to get more passionate about down-to-earth stuff like people, crops and livestock. Living, breathing things."

"And that makes you a better person than me?" she insisted, temper rising again. "More compassionate and caring? More human because your passions are more basic?"

"Different," he insisted tersely. "Not better or worse, just different. The world would be a damned boring place if we all shared the same passions."

His declaration mollified her somewhat, and she decided not to argue with him anymore. She'd spent a lifetime trying to explain herself to men, and she knew it was a waste of time.

They finished their meal in silence. He ate every bite she'd cooked and a couple extra pieces of toast. She was pleased that for once the food she prepared actually tasted like it was supposed to.

The coffee had stopped perking by the time she'd cleared the table, so she poured them both a cup and sat back down. Ryan thanked her, then pinned her with a steady, curious gaze.

"So what type of corporate battle sent you into hiding?"

She hesitated, no longer sure she wanted to share her concerns with him. His attitude seemed anything but supportive, and she didn't care for his acerbic tone.

"Sometimes an unbiased opinion can be invaluable," he pointed out more objectively.

He was right, and she knew it, so she decided to give him the details. "Besides my father, the company has three other executives—myself, my cousin Steven, and my dad's protégé, Geoffrey."

"What happens in case of tie-breaking decisions?"

"Dad has the final say in all decisions, but he's incredibly democratic about it. He won't back a decision he feels is wrong, but he'll go with the majority if he feels the decision has merit."

"A democracy with dictatorship?"

"A dictatorship that values the democratic process might be a better way to describe it," she explained. "My granddad founded the company, then Dad took the reins when he retired. The stockholders have always been content to leave all the decisions to him.

"Over the last few months, he's steadily given us more control. He's thinking about retirement and has been testing us all like we were newly hired employees. He's constantly pitting us against each other, and it's driving me crazy!"

"You just said you thrived on competition," Ryan reminded.

"Normally, I do, when it's outside competition. But I'm a team player when it comes to the company. I feel we should be expending our collective energy on developing stronger customer relations. Steven and Geoffrey are more interested in our international standings. They want to expand the whole focus of the company."

"Consolidation?"

Erica's mouth tightened. "First they want to sell off some of our smaller, less productive companies. The same ones that have been our bread and butter for years, I might add. Then they want to transfer some operations to Mexico and South America."

"Cheaper labor and increased production without the inconvenience of US labor laws," put in Ryan.

"Right, and I think it's highly unethical. I don't care what other big corporations are doing. And I don't care if the numbers prove we could double our annual profits. I feel we owe some loyalty to those companies who've helped us grow and thrive, even if they are more expensive to maintain right now."

Ryan nodded. "Your dad agrees with Steven and Geoffrey?"

Sipping her coffee, Erica kept her eyes shielded by her lashes. His question hit on the crux of the matter, and on one of her deepest disappointments. She assumed that since her dad promoted Geoffrey, he'd be siding with the men. His betrayal hurt so much that she couldn't even voice it aloud.

"So," prodded Ryan when she was quiet too long, "how does your dad stand on the issue?"

"I'm not sure. That's what worries me. Five years ago he wouldn't have considered it, but now I just don't know."

"So you decided to disappear for a few weeks? It doesn't sound like very good strategy to me."

She hadn't been thinking strategy when she'd left. She'd felt wounded and vulnerable, trying to protect herself until she could come to terms with her dad's decision.

"I took a leave of absence. We were all getting too emotional about the issue, and I figured a six week cooling down period would benefit the negotiations."

"And, in the meantime, show them how invaluable you are?"

The mockery was back in Ryan's tone, expunging her spurt of self-pity. She flashed him an annoyed glance. Her decision to take a leave hadn't been calculated, just purely emotional, but she'd cut out her tongue before admitting it.

"Damn straight, and it's working. Steven and Geoffrey are already whining about their increased workload. The customers aren't too happy, either."

That should have been satisfying, but it wasn't good business to antagonize customers. Erica only hoped she could smooth ruffled feathers once she was home again.

She and Steven had been researching a few Fortune 500 companies with the intention of proposing a merger. Their problems would be solved if Handlemen Industries, Ryersons Corporation, or the Tine-Williams Group were interested, but she hadn't had time to make a pitch to any of them.

"Interesting story," Ryan declared as he rose from his chair and stretched languidly. "But it doesn't explain why you decided on a working vacation rather than some island resort."

Her temper spiked again at the reminder. "Because they had the gall to tell me I couldn't survive on my own without good references. I told them I could and would do just fine without support from the firm, family or friends."

"So you went into hiding?"

"In a fashion," she admitted, collecting dirty dishes with agitated, jerky movements. "I didn't know exactly how I was going to survive, and I didn't want them watching me."

"Probably just as well they didn't know about Bubba's," he suggested, his tone once again teasing.

She put the dishes into the sink and turned to look him directly in the eyes. It was a mistake. She kept forgetting how his eyes mesmerized, how they could turn so swiftly into deep, churning pools of seduction. Weapons so powerful should be outlawed, she thought, finding herself totally distracted.

Irritation slowly gave way to the familiar heat he always generated in her.

Ryan moved closer, and she was besieged by an acute sensual awareness. He was dangerously attractive when he was playing the tease. His eyes glittered, breathtakingly gorgeous. Her heart thumped in reaction to his lazy, lopsided grin.

"Just as well," she agreed, nervously sucking her upper lip between her teeth.

His voice dropped an octave as his gaze settled on her mouth. "Bubba's served a purpose, but you won't add it to your résumé?"

Erica shook her head slightly. "No," she whispered as he narrowed the distance between them. The air deserted her lungs as the atmosphere between them crackled with heightened tension.

"No what?"

She fought to drag in a breath as he slipped his good hand to the curve of her neck. His fingers were hot and callused, searing her with sensation, but his touch infinitely gentle.

She had a hard time keeping track of the conversation. Her whole body swayed closer to the heat of his, like the pull of the tides. "No, I won't list Bubba's on my résumé."

"But yes, I can kiss you?" he asked, pulling her head toward his in sinfully slow motion.

She shuddered when his lips finally met hers. He brushed them back and forth as if to caress her from every angle. His teeth nibbled and his tongue traced, giving her the opportunity to experience the many textures of his mouth.

Pressing her hands flat on his chest, she flexed her fingers, kneading the taut flesh, enjoying the sensation of soft cloth over solid muscle.

"Mmm..." Ryan's murmur was one of pleasure as he shifted closer, trapping her between the counter and his body.

Erica shifted, too, aligning herself more fully against his lean frame. Impatient for the taste of him, she parted her lips and enticed him with the tip of her tongue. His reaction was swift as he accepted the invitation, thrusting his tongue into her mouth and groaning low in his throat as she caressed it with her own.

He tasted of coffee. He smelled uniquely male. He felt hard and unyielding as she melted against him. With only the pads of his fingers, he explored her face while deepening their kiss. His touch was light, yet it curled through her body on a ribbon of sensation.

His tongue went exploring, too. It swept across her teeth and into the hollows of her cheeks, then coaxed her tongue to dance. Erica didn't even think of refusing. She was totally bemused by his wholly focused exploration of her mouth.

He licked her lips gently when they needed to catch their breaths, and then sealed her mouth with his once again. She was sinking fast, tumbling like Alice down an endless tunnel. She didn't know where she would land, but she wasn't afraid. Ryan was with her.

The next time their lips parted, he drew back slightly, focusing his passion-hazed eyes on hers. She saw a reflection of herself and the same turmoil of emotion she was feeling, the same helpless yearning.

It was like nothing she'd ever experienced, an awakening when she hadn't even realized she'd been asleep. His touch, his taste, the feel of him was irresistible. She wanted more.

Grasping his head in her hands, she pulled it back down, taking his mouth and probing it as thoroughly as he'd done hers. Her tongue skimmed the smoothness of his teeth and did a slow, thorough search before sucking his tongue in increasing demand.

Ryan made a rough sound of hunger that echoed in her head and heart. She felt a thrill of feminine pleasure at her ability to both feel and arouse such need. The erotic power could become addictive. She couldn't seem to get her fill of him, either.

They shared another long, deep kiss, holding each other tight. Their bodies involuntarily strained for closer contact. Hearts thudded heavily against each other, pumping a river of desire through their veins.

It could have been minutes or hours later when the sound of a banging door finally penetrated the haze of passion. They slowly drew apart. Each of them knew Zack and Will were coming inside for their daily orders, yet neither was able to snap out of the sensual trance. Their gazes remained entangled, their breathing ragged as they struggled for control.

A tap at the kitchen door was followed by Will's voice. "Mornin' folks." When he didn't get an immediate response, he coughed, and added, "Would ya rather we come back later?"

Both men were openly staring when Ryan finally turned to them, partially shielding her as he raked a hand through his hair. "We're done eating," he said. "Grab some coffee if you want, and we'll head for the office."

They refused the coffee, hurried through the kitchen and headed down the hallway. Ryan gave Erica one last lingering look, and followed them.

She stood, dazed and trembling, and watched him go. When her legs threatened to buckle, she moved to the table and sat down heavily in a chair. For a few minutes, she stared at her unsteady hands and forced herself to take deep, calming breaths.

It was only a kiss. Not their first kiss, not even their most intimate embrace. So what in the world had just happened to her? Why were her insides quivering like Jello? Why was every nerve in her body humming with savage pleasure? How had a few simple kisses kindled such a fire in her soul?

She shook her head as if to rid it of unanswerable questions. It took a few more minutes and several slow, deep breaths before her body finally calmed. Then, by sheer force of will, she shook off the remaining effects of Ryan's attentions.

She didn't have time for this. She had an agenda. A corporate career to consider. Her home was in Chicago. She didn't belong here with a reckless cowboy and his passion for living things. He'd made that perfectly clear without actually saying the words. She was different, driven, lacking compassion for what he considered the most important things in life.

Their differences couldn't be more distinctive, their futures more diverse. On a scale of one to ten, their chances for a lasting relationship came in at a minus five. It was insane to consider becoming lovers. The physical attraction was already too muddled with emotion. Someone could get badly hurt. Maybe both of them.

Erica wasn't going to let it happen. Pulling herself together, she rose from the table and attacked the dirty dishes with a vengeance. Banishing thoughts of Ryan, she forced herself to concentrate on the conversation with her mother.

A short while later, all three men left the house to begin the day's chores. She didn't question Ryan's decision to join the others. He probably couldn't do much in the way of physical labor, but she knew he wanted out of the house. She imagined he was as anxious to put some distance between them as she was.

Last night, he'd shown her stacks of data that needed to be entered into the ranch files. She happily tackled that project next, finding comfort in the simple office routine. With luck, the job would keep her mind occupied most of the day.

Chapter Seven

On Friday of the same week, the men were having their morning planning session when they heard Erica screaming Ryan's name. All three shot out of their chairs and headed to the back of the house.

The kitchen was empty, but another high-pitched squeal led them through the porch to the backyard. They stopped abruptly when they saw the problem. Lying flat in the grass, Erica was being attacked by twelve roly-poly puppies.

"Stop!" said Erica, lifting one off her thigh only to have another replace it. "Don't do that," she repeated, then convulsed into giggles as the pups tickled her with their tongues and nipping teeth. She was nearly buried in energetic bundles of fur.

"Ryan! Do something!" she screeched when she saw them. "I need help!" Scooping two of the pups off her chest into the crook of her arms, she tried to sit up. Her attempts were foiled from behind as another pup tugged fiercely on her hair.

"Ouch, you little monkey." She collapsed onto her back again, gasping for breath and reaching for the pup that had his teeth tangled in her hair.

Ryan grinned at her predicament, the sound of her infectious laughter going straight to his heart. She looked happier and more carefree than he'd ever seen her. Thick, wild curls framed her lovely features and caught fire in the morning sun. Dew-sparkled grass cushioned her slim, athletic body.

His chest felt tight, full of some foreign emotion he was unwilling to analyze. The desire he'd spent the last few days trying to deny came rushing back with breath-stealing force. Sadie's pups were just a month old and in the mood to play. They usually stayed in the barn lot, but were venturing further each day. Apparently they'd caught Erica's scent and come to investigate the visitor.

"Hey, I'm under attack here," she reminded between giggles. "I could use some help."

"Can you guys round up the pups while I rescue the damsel in distress?" asked Ryan.

"Sure, boss," said Will.

Zack whistled for Sadie. Once she galloped into the yard, the babies lost interest in Erica and turned their attention to their mama and breakfast. Will and Zack grabbed a couple pups each and lead the whole family back to the barnyard.

Ryan went to Erica and looked down on her. She'd collapsed, spread-eagle, panting from exertion. Her chest rose and fell with each breath, offering a tantalizing view of plump breasts pressed against the thin fabric of her shirt.

He took his time studying her from breast, to stomach and long, bare legs. The weather had turned hot, so she wasn't wearing much. The gym shorts and T-shirt left a whole lot of bare skin to admire. He studied every delectable inch of it and then let his gaze roam back to her face.

"Some rescuer you are," she said, the words coming on a soft puff of air. "If those had been mad dogs, I'd be dead meat."

"They're just babies with baby teeth. It's your own fault. If you weren't so damn sweet, they wouldn't want to eat you."

"I could have been licked to death."

He chuckled, but a quiver of longing coursed through him. He wouldn't mind having a turn tasting her. He fantasized about exploring every sweet inch.

"I don't think we've ever lost any staff that way. There's a first time for everything, but I think you're safe."

"Safe maybe, but I've been slimed."

He threw back his head and roared with laughter while offering a hand. "Can I expect to be sued? Gonna tell the judge you suffered debilitating emotional damage from a sliming?"

Erica accepted his help, but swiftly pulled from his grip once she was standing. She shot him a grin while brushing grass from her clothes. "I'll keep it in mind. You suppose there's a statute of limitations on puppy dog tongue-tickling attacks?"

Ryan laughed again, enjoying her sense of humor as much as her sexy, tousled beauty. He wanted to pull her into his arms and kiss her breathless, but he still hadn't recovered from the last devastating kisses they'd shared.

He'd been so stunned by the power of those kisses that he'd been keeping a safe distance. Apparently she felt the same because they'd been avoiding unnecessary contact. Now she was giving him a warm, happy smile that made his pulse accelerate and his muscles constrict. Desire flared in him, nearly powerful enough to bring him to his knees. He shifted his gaze to the field beyond her while he fought for control.

He started to speak, but his throat was so tight he had to clear it and try again. "I was heading out to check the garden this morning. Want to come along?"

"Sure." She fell in beside him as he started across the yard. "Is the garden in that field behind the garage?"

For the past couple days, Ryan had been showing her the ranch, but there hadn't been time to see it all. "Yeah, I haven't taken you out there because it's been too wet."

"I was going in that direction, but I got waylaid."

"How'd they manage to knock you off your feet?" he asked, shooting her a glance.

"I made the mistake of squatting down to pet one, and then they all pounced at once. They're stronger than they look."

Ryan shook his head. "Sure, Red."

She responded with bubbly laughter that hit him square in the chest. It sent flames shooting through his body and pooling in his groin. He clenched his fingers into fists to keep from reaching for her. It made his broken hand ache, but the pain was nothing compared to the aching need.

The hunger he felt for her just wouldn't abate. He was familiar with physical attraction. He could handle that, but this was different. The emotional pull was every bit as strong as the physical. And that had him worried. Worried and wary.

He'd exhausted himself doing two-handed chores with one hand, but he still couldn't sleep at night. The battle for control was taking a bigger toll than he'd ever had to pay.

"Wow, this is a really big garden," Erica said as they moved to a fenced off area. "Did you plant it yourself?"

"With the help of a small seeding machine."

"I don't know one plant from the other. Tell me what everything is."

Her interest seemed genuine, so Ryan started at the far end of the garden. "There're ten rows of sweet corn. See how it's taller than the rest of the plants?"

"I recognized the corn, but it's about the only thing."

"Then there're peas and beans. You have to look closer to see the differences. Right now the weeds look like they're about to take over. It needs a lot of work since the rain."

As he explained, they walked the length of the garden, stopping to study the plants and distinguish weeds from vegetables. They finished with rows of tomatoes and peppers.

"What in the world will you do with all this food?" she asked. "There must be enough to feed a small army."

"The guys take what they want, and I have a friend in town who loves to preserve vegetables. She doesn't have a garden, so I supply the crop, she cans it and then shares it with me."

"Your own bartering system?"

"Exactly."

"Do you have to pull all the weeds by hand?" she asked after he'd leaned down to pull one very large one.

"I have a tiller to run between the rows, but it might be a little tough to run without two good arms."

"Can't someone help?"

"The staff's already shorthanded and overworked. I won't heap any more chores on them."

"I could help," she said, giving him a swift glance, then turning her attention back to the garden. "You'd have to show me how, but I'm a quick study," she reminded with a grin.

"You're already in charge of the house and the office."

"Piece of cake," she insisted, tossing her hair. "I'm ready to take on some new chores. Your neighbors supplied us with plenty of food, so I don't have to cook, and I'm finished with the paperwork you needed done."

Ryan studied her for minute. The wind was whipping her hair into a wild tangle and the sun was already turning her cheeks pink. She looked windblown and adorable.

"Weeding is dirty, sweaty work," he warned. "The tiller's a heavy piece of equipment and it takes brute strength to run."

"Are you telling me you don't think I can handle it, cowboy?" She turned to him, propping her hands on her hips and presenting him with a mutinous expression. He was beginning to recognize all the signs of her militant mode.

More than anything in the world, he wanted to lay her down in the soft warm grass and cover her body with his own. Just the thought had his hormones churning. More than temptation, she was a fever in his blood that nothing could cool.

To hide his reaction, he bent to lift a handful of garden soil. "I figured it would be too wet to till. We got a lot of rain, but this area drains fast. The sun and wind seem to have dried the worst of it. We can give it a try."

"We?"

"I can start the tiller and bring it here from the shed. I just can't run it through the rows. It takes two strong arms once the rotors are engaged."

Erica grinned, eyes dancing, and held up both arms, flexing well-toned muscles. "I'm small, but I'm mighty."

Ryan laughed again, shaking his head. He'd let her give it a try if for no other reason than to show her there were things she really shouldn't do.

"I'll go get the tiller. You can check out the closet on the back porch. You should be able to find some sunscreen, gloves, a long sleeved shirt and a hat."

Erica scrunched her nose, but didn't argue. She turned and headed toward the house. He watched her until she disappeared behind the garage, enjoying the view a little too much. Shaking his head in self-disgust, he went for the tiller.

In less than ten minutes, they returned. He grinned at the picture she made with her hair tucked beneath a floppy straw hat and a work shirt over her tee. Her long legs were still bare, and the sight brought to mind every story he'd ever heard about farmers' daughters.

He positioned the tiller at the end of a row, its noisy, rumbling engine making it necessary to shout instructions. When he was sure Erica heard and understood what she had to do, he stepped aside and let her take hold of the handle.

Then he roared with laughter.

The strong vibrations of the machine shook her entire body, making her look like a cartoon character that'd been zapped by lightning. Her eyes and mouth rounded, and she shot him a startled glance.

Their gazes met, his sending an "I told you so" message while hers said "you could be right". Then she began to laugh at herself. The sound rippled through the air and smacked him hard. Gone was the corporate persona. In its place was a sunny disposition and beautiful, spirited woman.

She enchanted him with the fun-loving, adventurous side of her nature. When he stood aside, she gripped the handle tighter and shifted the rotor tines into action. Then she held on for dear life as the tiller lunged forward, viciously clawing at the ground. Looking like a drunken sailor on a misguided mission, she plunged down the row.

The sky was clear and blue, the sun climbing higher as they worked. A light breeze kept it from being uncomfortably hot. The weather had been nearly perfect since the rains ended, and spring was in full bloom.

His broken arm had been a major setback, but hiring Erica had kept the setback from being a full-fledged catastrophe. The more she learned about the ranch, the more she wanted to know. Nothing daunted her. She faced each new challenge with an energy and enthusiasm that continually amazed him and his men.

She'd enslaved his staff by asking questions and listening intently to their answers, by allowing them to share their knowledge with her. She made each of them feel important.

She'd earned their respect by offering them hers, never belittling anyone or the duties they performed. It was easy to envision her as a dynamic, successful executive. She was hardworking, open-minded and willing to risk her own dignity for the chance to learn. She was totally out of her element and should have been a square peg in a round hole. Instead, she was a chameleon, ever changing, ever fascinating.

As they worked, Ryan's gaze followed her movements, scouring her features to make sure she wasn't getting too much sun or exhausting herself. He divided his time between attacking weeds and watching his city girl wrestle with the tiller. Keeping an eye on her had become his favorite pastime.

Nearly an hour passed before they stopped to rest. He knew Erica was going to ache in places she'd never known could hurt, but she refused to quit until the last row was finished. He finally stepped beside her and shifted the machine into idle, then pried her fingers from the handle.

"I think I've acquired a permanent tremor," she shouted over the din of the tiller's engine. "I'm not holding it anymore, but I'm still shaking."

"Occupational hazard," he declared, returning her grin. He couldn't remember ever smiling as much as he had today.

Erica swiped sweat from her forehead with the sleeve of her shirt, smearing dirt across her face. Ryan's smile widened. His newest employee didn't look anything like an uptight executive this morning. She just looked damned appealing.

Resisting the temptation to pull her into his arms, he grasped the tiller. "I'll show you where we keep it."

They slowly made their way past the garage to a smaller building where he parked the tiller and finally shut off the engine. The sudden silence made her laugh out loud.

"Wow, my ears are still ringing. I didn't realize how loud it was until it stopped. I might be permanently impaired."

"It passes," he teased, tilting the brim of her hat back so that he could see her eyes. "You did a great job on the garden. Thanks for the help. I couldn't have done it myself."

Erica's eyes lit with pleasure, and his pulse leapt, too. He wanted to kiss her so bad that he thought he might die from need, yet he didn't want to destroy the light-hearted mood they were sharing. He turned and pointed out the other equipment.

"This is where we keep the lawn mower, tiller, weed eater and all the other gardening tools and supplies."

Erica wandered over to the lawn mower and reached out to stroke the seat. "I've always wanted to drive one of these little tractors. When do we mow the lawn?"

He barked another laugh. The wistful tone of her voice amazed him. He couldn't believe she was drooling over his lawn mower.

"Forget about mowing today," he told her, touching her arm and guiding her out of the building. "I need to get the grass cut, but I think you've had enough sun for a while."

"I suppose," she grumbled, "but I could just take it for a test ride. I'm a very good driver."

"I'm sure you are, Red. Maybe tomorrow."

She looked ready to argue, but Zack interrupted them by shouting from the nearest barn. "Ryan, she's coming!"

Erica gave him a questioning look. "She who?"

"We have a mare about to foal. I told Zack to let me know when she went into labor. Wanna watch?"

"Will she mind?"

"I don't think so," he replied, tongue-in-cheek.

She slapped him on the arm. "Don't make fun, cowboy. How should I know anything about horses having babies?"

He laughed and grabbed her arm again, heading toward the foaling barn. He was inexplicably proud of her willingness to trust him and share his interests, even for a little while.

The barn was dark when they entered and it took a minute for their eyes to adjust to the change. They walked through the center aisle between rows of stalls to the end where Zack and their vet, Sam Jones, were tending the downed mare.

Zack was stroking the horse's neck and crooning to her in a low, soothing tone. Sam, a small, gray-haired man, was at the other end of the horse, preparing to help deliver her offspring. Ryan introduced them, and she explained that she'd never watched the birthing process of any animal, let alone such a huge one.

"Sugar's doin' fine," said the vet. "We're here in case she gets into trouble, but this is old hat for her."

"Her name is Sugar?" asked Erica, edging closer.

"No officially, but she has a fondness for sugar cubes," Ryan explained. "That's how she got her nickname."

He watched as Erica took in the sight, wondering what she was thinking as she studied the laboring mare.

"She seems to be breathing awfully hard."

"Birthin' babies is hard work, ma'am," said Sam.

"So I've been told," she murmured without taking her eyes from the horse's heaving, sweating body.

"Here comes the head." Sam said as he shifted to support the foal's emerging body.

Ryan missed the actual delivery. He was too engrossed in the play of emotions on Erica's face. He'd seen dozens of deliveries, but he'd never watched someone witness it for the first time. It touched him more deeply than the actual birth.

Her eyes were wide, her brow creased in concern. She gnawed on her lower lip as the mare shuddered and grunted with effort. When Sam pronounced the delivery a success, her eyes glistened and her expression filled with wonder. Tears promptly filled her eyes, turning them to sparkling gems and giving him a swift kick in the gut. At that point, he turned his attention to the newborn.

"A filly," pronounced Sam as he helped clean the baby. "She's a beaut. Sorrel with white fetlocks, just like mama."

"What's sorrel? Her color? And fetlocks?"

"Sorrel's reddish brown, like your hair. Fetlocks are the joints near her hooves. She's got white socks."

Zack and Sam moved out of the stall to allow the mother and baby a chance to bond. Ryan could see by Erica's widening eyes that the equine pair continued to amaze her.

"They're both trying to stand up!" she exclaimed in an anxious whisper. "Isn't it too soon?"

"It's normal for horses," he assured, watching Sugar rise to her feet and turn her attention to her newborn. Nudging the little one gently, she gradually urged it to its feet.

Erica laughed softly as the baby finally managed to stand on all four long, wobbling legs. "She looks like I felt when I was tilling," she whispered, tossing him a grin before shifting her attention back to the horses.

He returned her grin, but she didn't notice. She was totally absorbed in the drama being staged by mare and filly. As soon as the newborn could stand, she went in search of food.

"Good girl," Zack said quietly.

The filly found a teat and began to nurse, tentatively at first, and then with more vigor.

"Jeez, she's hardly two minutes old and already wanting to eat. Is that normal?"

"Yes, ma'am. That's what nature intended," said Sam. "Babies are born with the right instincts. Otherwise, we've got problems."

Erica's hold on his arm had gone from light, to gripping and back to light. Caught up in the miracle of birth, she'd reached out to him. He knew she'd be embarrassed when she realized it.

They'd been careful not to do much touching the last few days. Now he nudged her aside so the others could clean the stall. She finally glanced up and noticed how intently he was watching her. She quickly removed her hand.

"I don't suppose you ever get tired of watching that."

"Nope," he assured her, then lowered his voice so only she could hear. "It's one of those things I get passionate about."

She held his gaze for a minute, and then slowly nodded her understanding. They'd shared a few special minutes, and he knew she'd been deeply affected by the experience. It was a small step. He'd be a fool to believe it meant she could really understand his passion for the ranch and ranching.

Few women had ever accepted him for who he was without trying to change him. Erica wasn't likely to be the exception. The world he'd been happy to escape was the world where she thrived, the lifestyle that fired her passions.

They spent the afternoon doing a variety of small chores around the ranch, repairing a gate, cleaning tack and refilling water troughs. Erica took her first horseback ride to help him check some fences. She handled that as everything else, with enthusiasm and determination to do it well.

Between chores, she'd disappear for a few minutes and he eventually realized she was making regular checks on the little filly. The newborn fascinated her with each visit, and she swore it was growing bigger and stronger every hour.

When it was time to call it a day, they headed toward the house, but stopped when Erica spotted a rope swing hanging in a backyard tree. They spent a few relaxed, leisurely minutes with her swinging and him pushing one-handed.

Ryan couldn't ever remember enjoying a day so much. Maybe because he'd shared it with a special lady. He never tired of watching her or answering her questions. Her optimism and laughter enchanted him as little else could do. He'd never wanted a woman more in his life, and he decided the time had come to do something about it.

Chapter Eight

After her shower, Erica studied the meager offerings in her wardrobe and pulled out a sleeveless cotton dress. The bold turquoise and gold pattern looked good with her coloring, especially now that she'd acquired a light tan. Loose and flowing, the simple style fell to midcalf and was perfect for a warm spring evening.

It was going to be an incredibly romantic evening, she felt certain. She and Ryan had developed a special bond, a unique rapport that was new and thrilling. It was time to take their relationship to a higher level. Anticipation had the blood humming through her veins, making her giddy with excitement.

Someone knocked on the door just as she dropped the towel and slipped her dress over her head. Surprised, she turned toward the door as it swung open, and the man on her mind appeared in the doorway.

Lifting her hands to her hips, she chided, "Come right in. Please don't bother to wait for a response."

His unrepentant grin did crazy things to her pulse. Dressed in nothing but ragged cutoffs, he was six foot, two hundred pounds of magnificent, virile male. He crossed both arms over his broad chest and leaned casually against the doorjamb.

"I wasn't sure you could hear me knock," he reasoned.

"Which would mean I wasn't prepared to entertain guests." She mocked his stance by crossing her arms over her chest. The action drew his gaze to her unrestrained breasts.

She watched, her breath hitching, as his eyes darkened with pleasure. His gaze rose to snag hers.

"I'm not a guest," he insisted, his tone going husky, "just a cohabitant who wondered if you'd like me to grill some steaks for supper."

"You couldn't ask when I came downstairs?"

"I got lonesome and didn't want to wait."

"Lonesome?" Had he really missed her in the brief time they'd been parted? "I thought you might be getting sick of my company."

Ryan didn't respond, just shook his head slowly without losing eye contact with her. The expression in his gaze and on his ruggedly handsome features was of a restless male gone too long without a mate. He made no attempt to disguise his hunger from her, and it had little to do with food.

Erica could feel the strength of his need without him putting it into words. For days they'd maintained a moratorium on touching, kissing or anything that might heighten their physical awareness. That hadn't stopped the need from swelling into something stronger and sharper than they could ignore.

Now, everything about him from the heat in his eyes to the deceptively casual body language displayed a desire to end the self-imposed celibacy. She studied him intently, knowing that he'd decided they should become lovers. And soon. Maybe even right now. Her heart slammed against her chest at the thought.

"It could be a big mistake," she whispered softly, refusing to play coy.

Ryan didn't pretend, either. "Mistake or no mistake, I want you, and I think you want me just as much."

His gaze roamed slowly over her body from tousled, upswept curls to brightly painted toenails, and then back to her face. She felt the sexual pull from his uncensored perusal in every fiber of her being.

"I want to make love to you, I want to see and touch and taste every inch of your sweet, sexy body. Right or wrong, the need's so powerful that I'm tired of fighting it."

Erica would never have imagined that words alone could seduce her so effectively. Blood sang in her ears, her breasts swelled, nipples tightening, while warmth pooled low in her belly. The slow, steady thud of her pulse sent heat simmering through her body.

"I want you, too," she managed on a husky whisper, slowly bridging the distance between them until she stood within arm's reach. Tilting her head slightly, she locked her gaze with his and felt their mutual need stoke the desire even hotter.

It might be wrong to make love to a man who didn't avow his love first. It might be a mistake to give her body without offering her undying love, but Erica was beyond analyzing the rights and wrongs of it. She'd never wanted anyone in her life the way she wanted Ryan. She'd never felt anything as potent as the need he created within her. Nothing that felt so incredibly right could be wrong. They were confident, consenting adults.

"There's just one thing you should know," she started.

He put a finger to her lips, trying to still any confession she felt compelled to make. The small action pleased her, but she couldn't allow him to discourage this particular confession or he'd be furious with her later.

It was a big one and not so easy to admit. Her voice dropped to a whisper and hot color invaded her cheeks. She shoved the words through a desert-dry throat.

"I'm a virgin."

Ryan snatched his hand back as though she'd bitten it. She watched his eyes widen in amazement, then darken again with some emotion so hot and fierce it defied description. Resignation came next, resignation fraught with frustration and finally acceptance. He didn't say a word, but turned to leave.

Erica stilled him with a hand on his arm and looked directly into his eyes. "I'm a virgin, cowboy, for a lot of very private reasons, but it doesn't mean I'm totally inexperienced. I'm not a baby or an innocent, and I want you very much."

He closed his eyes, and she heard him suck in a tattered breath. She knew he was mentally weighing the risks and responsibility of being her first real lover. His body was taut with tension, so she decided to help him make up his mind.

Placing both hands flat on his chest, she began to caress him softly, learning the texture of smooth, tight skin over rope-hard muscle. Her fingers tangled in the tight golden curls, and then went searching for hidden treasure. When her nails raked his nipples, she felt his whole body shudder.

Ryan made a low, rough sound and grasped one of her wrists with his good hand. He used the broken arm to gently nudge her other hand off his chest. Erica didn't let the defensive actions deter her. With his arms holding hers apart, she could narrow the distance between them even further. Stepping very close, she sought a sensitive nipple with tip of her tongue.

The sound he made this time was little more than a feral growl rumbling from deep in his chest. His nipple hardened to a satisfying knot in her mouth, and she shifted to give similar attention to the other one. A shudder racked his body. He groaned and sunk his fingers into her hair, telling her without words that she'd managed to allay some of his concerns.

He nudged her backward until he could close the bedroom door, then wrapped both arms around her and pulled her close. She felt the crush of his chest against her breasts and the thick ridge of his arousal pressing into her stomach. Pure instinct made her arch her hips into the cradle of his.

Spreading his legs to better accommodate her, he slid one hand to her bottom and tugged her against his straining flesh. Erica wrapped her arms around his neck and dragged his head down for a long, searing kiss. There was no playful teasing, just fierce, raw hunger as their mouths locked and tongues plundered.

Sinking the fingers of one hand into his hair, she used the other to drag him closer, all the while rocking her hips against his in silent, pagan demand.

"Damn, Erica, you go straight to my head," Ryan gasped as their mouths parted slightly. "Are you sure?"

"Absolutely sure."

He hungrily nibbled her lips, his words sandpaper rough. "Then help me get out of these shorts."

"A little too tight?" she teased, capturing his mouth again while sliding her hands to the waistband of his shorts. His stomach quivered when her fingers slipped beneath the snap and unfastened it. His engorged flesh made short work of sliding down the zipper.

Erica lifted her hands to his waist and caressed the firm, hot flesh. Then she slid her hands around his back and slipped them beneath the fabric until she was clutching his tight rear end. He bucked his hips, grinding his arousal against her in urgent demand.

"You're killing me!" he accused roughly, breaking off another hot, wet kiss.

She gave him a tremulous smile. "You don't feel dead," she whispered while shoving his shorts and briefs off his hips. "You feel strong and aroused and very much alive!"

Ryan eased enough distance between them to step out of his clothes. The action had her sliding her hands around his hips and caressing his thighs. He took another step backward. Their gazes locked for another long minute. Chests heaved as they dragged in air. Both trembled with spiraling sexual tension.

"We have to slow down," he insisted gruffly. "And we need to discuss some options here."

Erica ran a finger down the middle of his chest, tickled his belly button and slid her caresses lower. He shuddered and grasped her hand as she enclosed his flesh in a firm, hot grasp.

"Options," he demanded in a strangled tone.

"What options? I'm not on the Pill, if that's what you mean."

He stilled, his gaze intense. "Does that mean we're going beyond heavy petting here? You'd better decide pretty quick."

Erica gave him what she hoped was a siren's smile. "No holding back, cowboy. I don't want petting. I want everything you have to give." She demonstrated the words by tugging free of his grasp and continuing her intimate caresses.

He sucked in air and gently shoved her back another step. "If you want peak performance, you'd better stop that right now, beautiful," he warned, shifting out of reach. He leaned down and pulled a foil packet from his cutoffs, tossing it to the nightstand before nudging her closer to the bed.

"Now, how about you get out of that dress?"

Erica bit her lip. It was one thing to totally expose his vulnerabilities, but altogether different to expose her own. Her confidence waned at the idea of stripping, but she could tell by the unholy gleam in his eyes that he wanted her to do just that.

"Don't get shy on me now," he coaxed, his gaze roaming her flushed features and locking on hers with persuasive softness.

She grasped the hem of her dress with both hands and began to gather the fabric in her fists. Lifting it slowly, she focused on his gorgeous nude body to distract herself from the reality of baring her own.

Cool air brushed her thighs, her belly and then her midriff, causing her to pause. Her breasts were already tingling and sensitive, but she forced herself to finish baring them. Ryan's hiss of pleasure as she tossed the dress aside made it worth the bravado it took.

His features were drawn tight with need as his gaze devoured her, stoking her arousal ever higher. His next demand scraped through his lips and sent a tremor down her spine.

"Now the panties."

Hands trembling, she slowly obeyed, sliding the scrap of fabric over her hips and off her legs, fully exposing herself. It took every ounce of courage she possessed to stand straight again, naked and defenseless before him.

She didn't know if it was the heat of embarrassment or the fever of desire that coursed over her body, but she grew hotter by the second. Ryan's scrutiny was slow and thorough and wildly exciting. She felt the touch of his admiring gaze on every inch of her body and a quaking need washed over her.

"Come," she coaxed, reaching out a hand to him as she sat on the edge of the bed. "Come closer."

He didn't need a second invitation. In the blink of an eye he was beside her, pressing her backward onto the mattress then stretching alongside of her. He kept his casted arm above her head, while using the other to cup her chin and lift her face.

He brushed adoring kisses on her forehead, her temples and her cheeks. He kissed the sensitive curve of her neck, her chin and both corners of her mouth. When Erica could stand it no longer, she grasped his head and guided his mouth to her own, moaning wantonly as he finally took it in a kiss filled with aching need.

Their tongues dueled, then tangoed, and Ryan slanted his mouth to fit more fully over hers. She clung to him, loving the taste and feel of him. No other man's kisses had ever inflamed her this way. No man had ever made her feel so restless and impatient and needy.

They gasped for breath when their mouths finally parted, but he wasted no time in furthering his caresses. He slipped lower in the bed and kissed a burning trail of fire down her throat to her breasts. Cupping one gently in his hand, he kneaded the firm flesh, worshipping the exquisite feminine form.

Next, he lapped at it with his tongue, then repeated the kneading and lapping on the other breast, sending sharp bites of sexual tension shimmering to the center of her body.

Erica clutched at his head, her fingers twining through thick locks of hair as he teased her nipples until they hardened into tight buds. His tongue was hot and wet and he stroked and licked until she thought she'd go out of her mind.

"Ryan, please!"

He bathed one nipple with his tongue while rolling the other with his thumb. Then, looking into her eyes, he smiled knowingly, wickedly, until she tugged his head to her breast.

"Tell me what you want, sweetheart."

"Your mouth," she whispered in a breathless pant.

He didn't make her wait, but caught a nipple and sucked it deeply into his mouth, drawing a low, keening moan from her. He feasted, taking his time and driving her wild, then treated the other breast to the same assiduous, unhurried attention.

Erica didn't think she could stand much more of his erotic caresses. Her lungs were tortured from heavy breathing. Her blood raced like molten fire through her veins, her breasts were swollen and throbbing, and his wickedly pleasing mouth just kept stoking the ache that pulsed at the core of her.

When she was sure she couldn't bear any more, his hand slid over her stomach and slipped between her legs. She convulsively tightened her thighs against the invasion.

"Shh, sweetheart, don't go tense on me now," he coaxed. "You're so sexy and responsive. Relax and let me love you."

Erica's throat was too tight to formulate a verbal response, but she admonished herself and slowly relaxed her muscles. He slid up far enough to give her another long, lingering kiss as his fingers explored sensitive territory.

She gasped as he touched her most intimate flesh, causing another tidal wave of heat to wash over her. She arched off the bed, but then he was kissing her again, soothing with his mouth while his fingers stimulated ultrasensitive nerve endings.

"So hot and wet," Ryan groaned against her lips. Their gazes met, mirroring a wild tumult of emotion. Erica knew she must look as feverishly aroused as he did and a whole lot more unsure of herself, but she was beyond caring.

He held her gaze as he slid one finger, then two, more deeply. She gasped, first withdrawing, then writhing against him in primitive demand.

"That's the way, sweetheart. Move with me. Open up for me." His voice was low and strangled with tension. "I'm about to die with needing you, but I don't want to hurt you."

He dropped his head to her breast again and sucked a nipple deeply into his mouth. Erica felt her body draw tight between the two intimate caresses. His mouth suckled while his fingers and thumb stroked her to new heights of need.

"Ryan!" Clenching her fingers in his hair, she pleaded hoarsely, shifting restlessly against the onslaught of escalating pleasure. "Please, Ryan, please!"

His fingers stroked deeper, harder, while he lifted his head and captured her mouth with a kiss that seared her soul. Seconds later he swallowed her hoarse cry of satisfaction as she tumbled over the edge. She collapsed, trembling and depleted, sure that her muscles had turned to mush.

Ryan knew better. He reached for the condom and sheathed himself, then slid one arm under her hips. Spreading her legs, he settled between them and then stole another kiss from her quivering lips. The taste was an aphrodisiac itself.

Next he gently licked each pouting nipple, feeling Erica still, and then quiver anew at the light caresses. Beautiful. Flushed with satisfaction and still trembling with the aftermath of sexual release, he found her incredibly beautiful and so damned desirable he thought he'd explode with wanting.

Needing to be inside of her more than he needed his next breath, he pressed closer and felt her stiffen. Despite her bold talk and sophisticated foreplay, she had to be a little anxious.

"Look at me, Erica," he demanded.

Her lashes swept up and her lovely sparkling eyes met his, eyes as bright and shiny as precious gems. He couldn't begin to decipher the chaos of emotions whirling in them.

"Last chance to bail. Are you sure?" he forced himself to ask, praying she wouldn't deny him now.

She nodded, but that didn't satisfy the need churning in him. It was an emotional need as sharp and urgent as the physical. "Tell me what you want. Make me a believer," he commanded roughly.

Clasping his face in her hands, she gently stroked his cheeks with her thumbs, lifting her hips to rock against him.

"I want to make you a part of me, cowboy," she murmured against his lips. "I want to know what it's like to have a real lover who wants me as desperately as I want him."

Then she thrust her tongue into his mouth and lifted herself so that he could join their bodies in the most elemental of ways. He didn't need any further encouragement.

Surging forward, he felt the pressure of resistance and slowly but steadily deepened his penetration. Then he was groaning with savage pleasure as her body accepted him, enfolding him in hot, gripping silk. Nerves strung taut, muscles quivering, he strained to still his convulsive movements until she'd adjusted to the size and feel of him. He dropped his head onto her forehead, breathing raggedly, and fought for control.

It seemed to take an eternity, but she finally began to arch against him in tentative demand. Then he lost all control, surging into her with powerful thrusts that made her his as completely and irrevocably as was possible.

His. She was his and only his. She'd given him the most special gift a woman could give—her trust. She'd allowed him an intimacy no other man had shared. Possessiveness hit him with the same thundering force as the near paralyzing climax.

Body shuddering, he sagged against Erica, but her breathing was as labored as his. After a few seconds, he found the strength to support his weight, resting his forehead against hers again while they fought for air. It took several minutes to muster more energy.

"Awesome," he whispered when he could speak again.

"Totally," Erica echoed huskily.

She sounded as shaken as he felt. Being a virgin could explain the intensity of her response, but not his. He didn't live like a monk. He'd had his share of sexual encounters, but nothing, absolutely nothing, could compare to what they'd just shared.

Lifting his head, he looked into her passion-clouded eyes and felt another jolt of hot sensation. This one came with instincts stemming from a different kind of virgin territory. He didn't want to go there. His lady wouldn't appreciate the sentiment.

Exhausted, they dozed, but Ryan woke with a jerk when he realized she was bearing the brunt of his weight. He tightened his grasp on her and rolled onto his back, pulling her onto his chest. Erica accidentally hit his cast with her elbow, and then looked at him with wide, worried eyes.

"Sorry, I didn't hurt you, did I?"

He smiled and shook his head, then lifted a hand to caress her cheek. "I should be asking you that. Did I hurt you?"

He loved the way she blushed. It made her features soften endearingly and tempted him to kiss her again. Before she could formulate a reply, he was sealing her lips with his, teasing her with playful thrusts of his tongue, and enticing her to play.

As always, she rose to the challenge, nibbling on his tongue and stroking it with her own. Their mouths locked tighter and the kiss deepened. She wriggled, snuggling closer, shifting her weight and brushing her breasts across his chest.

Ryan groaned and felt the blood start to hum through his body in renewed vigor. With no more than a kiss and a wiggle she made him hot again. He broke off the kiss and stared into her eyes.

"You never answered my question," he said.

Erica flicked her tongue across his lips and his muscles clenched. He stroked her shoulders and the smooth curve of her spine, cursing the plaster that kept him from feeling all of her with both hands.

"What question?" she mumbled and nibbled his chin.

"I asked if I hurt you."

Now she was using her teeth on the curve of his shoulder, making goose bumps race down his body. He shuddered and flexed his fingers against the supple flesh of her hips. When she still didn't answer, he clutched her sweet little tush.

"Erica?" A groan forced her name from his lips.

"I'm busy," she said, returning her attention to his nipples. Her wicked tongue had already teased them erect, now she sucked at them with unwavering eagerness.

"I realize that," he hissed, wishing he had the use of both hands. He wanted to drag her up his body and bury his face in her breasts. Then he'd show her a thing or two about arousal.

Attempts to gently dislodge her were a waste of time. She straddled his thighs and refused to budge, thwarting his half-hearted effort to shift her onto her back again.

"You best slow down," he warned as she blazed a trail of hot, wet kisses down his stomach, tying his muscles in knots. When she continued to ignore him he resorted to brute strength. Cupping the back of her head in his palm, he dragged her slowly back up his body until they were eye to eye again.

"You can't be goin' there, sweetheart," he drawled. She had him so excited his blood raced through quivering limbs while his chest heaved with the effort to keep it pumping.

"Why not?"

If ever he'd seen a temptress, this redhead took the prize. Her hair in a riotous tumble, face flushed and eyes gleaming, she stole his breath and rattled his composure.

"I don't have any more protection with me."

She frowned. "Aren't cowboys always supposed to be prepared?" she insisted, then went back to scattering soft, teasing kisses on his nose and cheeks.

"That's the Boy Scouts."

"Oh, shoot!"

Her gaze met his again, gleaming with laughter until he cupped her breast in the palm of his hand and stroked the tip with his thumb. He felt her whole body tighten against him.

"Such beautiful breasts," he whispered.

Her answer was little more than a breathy whisper. "And you have a thing for breasts."

"I do. I'm a little hindered with the cast, but I want a whole lot more time to worship yours. How about we get dressed and eat something, then spend the rest of the night in my room?"

"Where you have lots more protection?"

Chapter Nine

Erica woke just before dawn the next morning and found herself snuggled against Ryan's hard, warm body. Her backside curled, spoon fashion, against his front side. She loved the feel of him wrapped around her and the way their bodies melded together into one very compatible entity.

The thought of being so totally in tune with another human being had her doing a lot of soul-searching and reevaluating of her life. As she got to know Ryan better, she learned more and more about herself, felt things she'd never imagined herself capable of feeling and doing.

A smile curved her lips and her eyes drifted closed again as she savored images of what they'd shared. She'd never thought of herself as insatiable, yet last night had been truly incredible. Ryan had destroyed every single inhibition she'd ever harbored and replaced them with a wondrous knowledge of how perfectly two people could complement each other.

Memories of their night of loving had her shifting restlessly. Within seconds, she felt his big body responding to her movements. Her smile widened, her pulse kicked into high gear, and she rocked her hips against him provocatively.

"Good morning to you, too, darlin'."

His deep voice whispered against her ear just before his mouth settled on the curve of her neck. He sucked gently, sending shivers of excitement over her. Wrapping his arms more fully around her, he brushed his fingertips against her breasts, bringing the peaks to erect attention. She sucked in a ragged breath as heat spiraled through her and settled in the pit of her stomach.

"Ryan!" His name escaped her in a rush of air.

"Ready and willing," he murmured, rubbing his aroused flesh against her in demand. "Your wish is my command."

Curled with her back to him, Erica could only reach his thigh. She stroked the hair-roughened skin, then slid her thigh over his, wordlessly coaxing him to join their bodies.

Combined moans of pleasure echoed in the quiet of the morning until excitement gave way to breathlessness. Their bodies, acutely sensitive after a night of loving, moved in perfect harmony, eagerly seeking and finding sweet satisfaction.

Then they dozed.

The next time Erica opened her eyes, sunlight was beginning to stream through the window. Ryan stood beside the bed, already showered and dressed. He leaned down to plant a kiss on her lips.

"Will and Zack will be in soon, so I'll go start the coffee. You can join us or spend the day in bed." He brushed a thumb lightly over her cheek and then cupped her face in his hand. His eyes were warm with admiration and deep contentment.

"I know you didn't get much sleep last night, but I can't say I'm a bit sorry."

His lips found hers again. The sheet fell to her waist as Erica locked her arms around his neck, relishing the feel of his hard chest against her tender breasts. He deepened the kiss and wrapped one arm around her bare shoulders to pull her closer. They kissed until they were both panting for air.

His voice shook on a husky growl. "You're a temptress."

"And you're a fantastic lover," she replied, eyes bright with adoration.

Ryan grinned. "I'm glad you think so, Red, because I'd like to do a repeat performance tonight."

"Is that so?" she teased. "What about sleep?"

"We'll take long naps in the afternoon."

Erica smiled and gave him another kiss. When he released her, she slid back onto the bed, and he turned toward the door.

"I put Trudy's breakfast casserole in the refrigerator to thaw last night," she told him. "If you stick it in the oven, we can eat as soon as I'm out of the shower."

"Sounds good to me," he said, opening the door. "Not as good as spending the whole day in bed with you, but that would cause a lot of speculation and gossip."

"I imagine it would," she agreed, giving him a grin as she pulled the sheet up to her neck.

Ryan frowned. "You're not going to get all uptight and modest, are you? If so, I'll say the hell with gossip and spend the day working on those inhibitions of yours."

Erica laughed throatily, cajoling an answering grin from him. "I don't have a modest bone left in my body, so you needn't worry. I'm not likely to forget anything about last night."

"That's a relief. I thought I might have to start from scratch again," he declared, giving her a wink as he stepped out the door and drew it closed behind him.

She listened to his footsteps fade down the hall, and then slowly climbed out of bed. Donning the dress she'd tossed aside hours earlier, she headed upstairs to shower in her own room. As water poured over her body, her thoughts whirled with images of the night they'd just spent.

She'd never let any man get as close as she'd let Ryan, nor even known two people could be so attuned to each other, both emotionally and physically. Most of her life had been an uphill battle for independence in her mother's social world and for respect in her father's business world.

There hadn't been time or energy left over for developing personal relationships. She'd only had one serious relationship since college and that had fizzled when her boyfriend decided he didn't want to play second fiddle to her career.

As she stepped from the shower and quickly dried herself, she wondered yet again, how long-term a relationship with Ryan could be. They lived in two totally different worlds, and she'd be leaving his in a couple more weeks. Neither of them would consider relocating. Of that she was certain. They hadn't discussed commitment last night. They'd just reveled in the joy of getting to know each other more intimately.

Erica told herself it didn't matter. She didn't want or need commitment. She wanted to experience as much pleasure as possible from an affair with a gorgeous, exciting man and not worry about the future. Even if the thrill lessened by the time she left, she'd have the memory of a once-in-a-lifetime fantasy.

Women did it all the time.

Or so she told herself as she dressed in dark blue gym shorts and a thin, matching T-shirt. After brushing her hair into a ponytail, she hurried downstairs. When she passed the office, the hum of male voices assured her that the men were still involved with their morning briefing.

The aroma of freshly brewed coffee lured her toward the kitchen. A quick check of the oven confirmed that the casserole was browning nicely, so she poured herself some coffee. She was leaning against the countertop, sipping at the hot, strong brew when Zack emerged from the office.

They exchanged smiles and greetings. "Coffee's ready if you'd like a cup," she said.

"No thanks, I've had my quota for the morning. Any more and I'll have worse jitters than the colt I'm trying to train."

Her innate curiosity kicked into gear. The ranch and its workings intrigued her, especially the horses. They were such fascinating creatures. The staff didn't seem to mind answering her questions, so she kept asking.

"Do you have to break the wildness out of them like I've seen on TV? You try to ride, and they keep bucking you off until one of you gives up?"

"It's important to earn a horse's trust before getting on his back. If he trusts you, he's not apt to grind you into the dirt," he explained with a rare grin.

Erica laughed softly, noting how the harsh lines softened when he relaxed enough to smile. He was one of the most uptight men on the ranch, but Ryan said he was great at his job.

"He still may not want you on his back, but he isn't as likely to seek retribution, huh?" she surmised.

They were sharing another laugh as the others entered the kitchen. Erica saw Ryan shoot a glance from Zack to her, and then his expression tightened.

"I thought you wanted an early start with that colt," he said to Zack, his tone sharper than she'd ever heard. "Shouldn't you get busy?"

An abrupt silence fell as the two men stared at each other. Zack's expression smoothed into a blank mask, while Ryan's remained tight and belligerent. The tension was palpable, making Erica wonder what in the world had happened between them.

"I guess I better get started," the foreman said, slapping his hat on his head. He moved toward the door with Will following. Both nodded to Erica, and she bid them a good day.

When the porch door slammed, and they were out of earshot, she demanded an explanation. "What was that all about? Why did you start snarling at Zack?"

Ryan raked a hand through his hair. "Damned if I know. The sound of you two laughing just hit me like a sucker punch."

Her mouth gaped open in astonishment. "You snarled at Zack because of me? You were jealous?"

"Yeah." He seemed equally shocked by the idea.

"So you were doing a little male posturing? Being a possessive, territorial, chauvinistic jerk?" she admonished.

His frown deepened as though the concept was totally foreign to him. "I suppose that's what I was doing. I'll apologize to him later. I guess I am feeling territorial where you're concerned. Is that surprising?"

Setting her cup on the counter, she slowly shook her head while considering his question. "I'm not sure. I've never had anyone act so possessive about me. It's a little flattering and a little unsettling. I don't think I'd care for much of it."

Ryan stepped near her and slid a hand behind her neck, tilting her head and drawing her close. "I can't say I'm real comfortable with the feeling, either. But then I've never experienced anything like we shared last night." The pitch of his voice dropped to a sexy rumble. "I guess it'll take some getting used to."

Erica felt herself melting. She badly wanted to believe what they'd shared was extraordinary for him, too.

"I guess it will," she agreed softly.

"I hope you don't mind the staff knowing about us. Between my posturing and the hickey on your neck, I think the cat's out of the bag. Zack won't say a word, but Will's not quite so close-mouthed."

The brush of his fingers on the back of her neck sent a shiver over her. She hadn't noticed a mark, but his touch reminded her of the way his mouth had caressed her earlier. The memory warmed her.

"I'm sorry," he said, dropping a tender kiss on the bruise. "I forgot how sensitive your skin is. I didn't mean to hurt you."

They stared into each other's eyes for a few pulsing heartbeats, then Ryan whispered, "That reminds me. You never told me if I hurt you the first time. I wanted to be gentle, but you had me so excited I lost my head."

She grasped his face in her hands and drew his mouth to hers. "I thought my responses were answer enough," she insisted, giving him a long, coffee-coated kiss that expressed her feelings better than words.

They were slow getting to work that morning and all the days that followed. The week was filled with discovery. Erica learned about ranching and opened herself to a whole realm of new experiences. Ryan basked in the pleasure of having a partner to share everything with—his ranch, his work, his lovemaking.

The time wasn't spent in perfect harmony. They were too strong-willed to agree on everything, yet they quickly realized the advantages of kissing and making up. They argued religion, politics and financial management. Although they disagreed frequently, they did it with steadily increasing respect for each other's opinions.

Erica continued to email her associates in Chicago. The business world was too much a part of her life to ignore, so she depended on the Internet for updates and information.

She also emailed her assistant, Janet, and asked for a discreet background check on Ryan Havens, feeling a little guilty, yet wanting to know anything and everything about him. He was far more astute about corporate policies than most the men she'd worked with in Chicago. It seemed strangely out of character for a ranch manager. A couple other things he'd mentioned piqued her curiosity.

The information Janet unearthed stunned her, to say the least. "You're absolutely sure?" she typed in a message.

"No doubt about it. Ryan Havens is Joel Ryerson's half brother."

"THE Joel Ryerson of Ryerson Corporation?"

"The same one you researched earlier in the year. Remember the brother who lives in Wyoming? He's considered reclusive, but a financial wizard?"

"Ryan Ryerson."

"Ryan Havens. We had the wrong name in our files. He's a half-brother. The ranch he runs is a family holding."

"Thanks," Erica signed off and stared into space, trying to come to terms with the amazing revelation. Suddenly, Ryan's whole attitude made sense and several pieces of his personality puzzle fell into place.

Her heart sank, her stomach roiling. Ryan, her Ryan, was Joel Ryerson's brother. When she'd left Chicago in an emotional tizzy, she'd headed to Wyoming because it was Janet's home state. She'd heard her assistant talk about the simplicity of life, which she'd desperately needed at that point.

What in the world was she going to do? She couldn't tell Ryan how she'd learned the truth. He'd be furious if he knew her company had been researching his family's firm with hopes of merger. He'd accuse her of stalking him or corporate espionage or something equally appalling.

He obviously didn't want her to know that his family owned a Fortune 500 corporation. In all their time together, and all their business discussions, he'd never hinted at his other career. Maybe he kept it a secret from the ranch staff and his neighbors. Or maybe he just thought of her as a passing fancy, unworthy of his trust. That stung.

*****

On the final Monday of her leave, she placed a call to her mother and got her father instead. The sound of his voice brought a rush of conflicting emotion. She'd missed him, but didn't know if she could talk to him without getting emotional and losing her cool.

She adored her dad and had spent her life trying to emulate him. A lot of men in his position would have bemoaned the lack of a son to follow in his footsteps. Her dad had always taken pride in her accomplishments. Until a few weeks ago, she'd thought he was grooming her to take over the company. His attitude prior to her leaving home had seemed totally out of character, and had shaken her confidence to the core. She hadn't just taken a leave from her professional life, but from her personal life, as well.

"Hello, Dad." The tightness in her throat annoyed her, but she couldn't seem to dislodge it.

"Erica, it's so good to hear your voice, honey. Your mother and I have been worried about you."

Sitting at Ryan's desk, she twisted the phone cord with nervous fingers and concentrated on keeping her voice steady. Her response sounded terse, but she couldn't help it.

"I told Mother I'm fine."

"I know what you've told your mother, but it hasn't been very comforting. We can't imagine how you're surviving."

"I'm an intelligent adult, Dad. I have a job and I'm living quite comfortably."

"You could at least tell us where you are."

"It doesn't make much difference. My leave of absence will be over in a few days." A pang of regret came with the acknowledgment, but she quickly suppressed it. Panic threatened every time she thought about the rapidly approaching deadline.

"You'll be home soon?"

She tried to ignore the relief in his tone. It had never been her intention to worry her parents. She knew they loved her and were concerned for her welfare. That had never been in doubt. What bothered her were her dad's true feelings about her future in respect to the business.

"I'll be home sometime next week."

"You have enough money?"

"Yes, Dad." Her impatient response met with a short silence. Then her dad's tone grew uncharacteristically soft.

"We've missed you, both at home and at work. You're still our sunshine, you know. The house is too quiet. The office is dull and boring. I didn't realize how much I depended on you for morale until you were gone. I guess that was your intention, huh? Teach the old man a lesson?"

Erica's heart thudded at his softly spoken questions, and she gripped the phone cord harder. She'd left because she'd been hurt. There had been no carefully orchestrated plan.

"That wasn't my intention. I just needed to get away."

"Because of Geoffrey's promotion?"

Her throat got tight again. She'd perceived his decision as a lack of faith in her abilities, and wasn't sure she could talk about it. It had shaken her badly.

Clearing her throat, she replied, "I worked harder than Steven or Geoffrey for that promotion."

"But you made the critical mistake of letting them both take credit for your work," he added in reproach. "I'm only beginning to realize just how much credit they've been taking and how much work you were doing."

His answer stunned Erica into silence. Her pulse raced as she considered all the implications of his words.

"So what now? Should I be preparing a résumé? Because I promise you I will not work well with Geoffrey if he starts ordering me around and playing boss man."

"I've given it a lot of thought and decided to give you and Steven promotions, as well. It's not uncommon to have more than one vice president. You'll each be in charge of areas where you excel. You'll be VP in charge of client relations."

Tears filled Erica's eyes, and she swiped at them as a heavy weight lifted from her heart. Her dad was trying to make things right. His effort, more than the promotion, meant the world to her.

"Erica? You still with me? Your mother has hounded me day and night since you left, lambasting me for being so dense. Please tell me you'll be home and back to work soon."

She finally found her voice again. "I'll be home soon and back to work."

"I planned to apologize, but I was hoping to do it in person, not long-distance on the telephone."

"Well, I'm glad you did. Now maybe I can come home with fewer worries. I thought maybe you wanted to get me completely out of your hair and leave the company."

"Never!" he exclaimed gruffly, and then tempered his response. "Well, never very far out of my hair, anyway. I want you to be happy, but I certainly don't want to lose your executive skills."

Erica laughed, her spirits soaring. "I'm glad to hear it."

"And I'll be glad when you get home. Can't you cut your leave short or are you committed to another job?"

Her breath caught at the suggestion. A week ago she might have considered it, but not now. No how, no way. She didn't want to think about leaving Ryan. The time would come soon enough, and she'd deal with it, but not a minute sooner.

"I'm committed here," she replied.

He didn't press. "Then I'll look forward to seeing you next week. I'll tell your mother you called and the two of you can talk later. Don't you forget that we miss you."

"I miss you, too."

"I'm forgiven?"

"You're forgiven," she said lightly. "Love you, bye bye."

Her dad returned her love and they broke the connection. Erica slowly replaced the receiver, her smile deep and satisfied. She adored her dad, and her heart felt lighter now that they'd cleared the air between them.

"Must have been some conversation to make you all dreamy-eyed. I take it that wasn't your mother."

Startled by the unexpected sound of Ryan's deep voice, Erica glanced toward the doorway. He stood with a shoulder braced against the door. In his usual tight-fitting jeans and shirt, he looked lean, sexy and a little bit dangerous.

She rested her elbows on his desk and braced her chin in both hands. Then she gave him a smile of wide-eyed innocence.

"You're wearing that possessive, territorial look again."

He stiffened. His eyes narrowed, and his expression grew tighter. "What of it?"

"I think I'm getting kinda used to it," she said. "Should I ask what caused it this time or have you been eavesdropping?"

"I heard the tail end of your conversation. Who's the guy you've forgiven and still love?"

She decided not to give him a direct answer, but to let him sweat it out a little longer.

"I think you might have gotten the wrong impression, but you're in luck. I'm in a really good mood. If you'd like to come over here, I'll share my news."

He continued to scowl. "You're in my chair."

She stood and hopped up on the edge of his desk, emptying his chair. Then she gave him a come-hither smile over her shoulder and patted his seat with her bare toe.

Ryan shoved himself from the door and slowly crossed the distance between them. She loved watching him move, his long, lazy stride and the poetry of motion in his panther-like grace. They maintained eye contact until he moved behind the desk and sat in his chair. Then Erica tugged him closer so that her calves were straddling his thighs.

Heat surged through her as soon as they touched. It was always the same. He got near and her hormones went haywire. She watched his eyes reflect the same reaction, and felt a surge of feminine triumph.

"The guy on the phone?" Ryan prompted.

His tone held a grim note, but his expression was less forbidding. He shifted the chair so that he could slide his arms around her waist and pressed his face against her breasts.

"I can't think when you distract me like that," she insisted, the feel of him stealing her breath. She ran her fingers through his hair and tugged his head backward so she could see his eyes. "That was Dad. I called Mother and he answered, so we cleared the air a little. I left home with some hard feelings, but he made everything better."

"Your dad?"

"My dad," Erica assured, feeling him gradually relax against her. "Does that soothe the possessive jerk in you?"

"For now," he said, lifting her off the desk and onto his lap. He planted a row of kisses up her throat until his mouth hovered over hers. "Any other men in your life?"

"Besides you?" She flicked her tongue against his lips.

A low, rumbling growl vibrated from his chest to his throat. "Besides me."

"I work in a man's world," she reminded. "There are lots of other men in my life."

Ryan nipped her chin with his teeth in punishment for evading his question. It tickled, and she giggled.

"Geoffrey, one of our executives, thinks he'd make me a perfect husband, but there's nothing serious between us."

"Nothing serious means nothing physical?" he prodded.

"You certainly are nosy for someone who never shares any details about himself. Communication is a two-way street."

Erica gave him the perfect opening to discuss his private life and second career. She badly wanted him to tell her about his family and the connection with Ryersons. His confidence and trust had become even more important to her than the promotion she'd just been promised.

"I'm a simple man, and you know plenty about me," he insisted. "My parents and only brother live in New York. I run this ranch, and it's my greatest passion. That's all there is."

"That's like saying the Grand Canyon is deep, cowboy," she chided, mentally coaxing him to give her more details about Ryersons before the whole situation blew up in their faces. "It doesn't even scratch the surface."

"Is that right?" He kissed her neck, sending goose bumps over her. "I like your silk. You should wear it all the time."

She'd spent the morning outdoors, but Ryan had ordered her in during the heat of the day. She'd showered and changed into a blue silk pantsuit while her other clothes were in the wash.

"It's not too practical for housework and cooking," she argued, clutching his face in her hands and stealing a kiss.

"It's perfect for making love," he murmured against her mouth. He massaged her spine, rubbing the silk against her flesh in an erotic caress. "At least it would be if you weren't wearing anything under it."

"What a shocking suggestion!" she teased, her lips flirting with his until he sealed them with another kiss. And another and another. Their arms tightened around each other, entwining their bodies intimately close. She forgot all about secrets and corporate connections, too far gone to care.

Then someone began pounding on the front door.

Chapter Ten

Ryan growled at the interruption, even though he knew he shouldn't be seducing Erica in the middle of a busy afternoon. He'd come in the house to check a vet record for one of the horses. Zack needed the information, but overhearing her phone conversation had sidetracked him.

Now he was aroused and didn't want to be bothered by anyone. He'd never known a woman who could light his fire as fast and often as his Erica could. The more he had of her, the more he wanted. The need just didn't abate, but the rest of the world kept intruding and it frustrated the hell out of him.

Another knock sounded, this one a little louder.

"You'd better answer that. It's probably a neighbor bringing food and our supply is getting low," she teased. "Ignoring it could mean depending on my cooking again." She slid off his lap before he could protest. Ryan scowled, and she gave him a flirty smile.

"Later," he threatened huskily. "When I come in for supper, I'll show you a whole new appreciation of silk."

"Promises, promises," she taunted, adeptly sidestepping his outreached arms. "We'd better go see who's here."

Just then, they heard the front door open and a woman's voice calling through the house.

"Hello! It's Katlyn. Anybody here?"

Ryan tensed as he recognized the voice. He could hardly believe his ears, yet the sweet familiarity of it brought a rush of pleasure. He lunged from the chair and strode down the hall. The sight of his lovely, long-time friend warmed his heart.

"Katlyn! How the hell are you?" he asked, grabbing her in a bear hug. "Long time, no see. Should you be running around?" It had only been a couple weeks since the birth of her baby.

She returned his hug and then stepped back to give him a brilliant smile. "I was going stir-crazy at the house, and Jared took pity on me. He had to see Will about getting some special shoes made for one of the horses, so I tagged along. I hope you don't mind the unannounced visit."

"Since when did you need an invitation?" he asked. They'd known each other since grade school, and had been as close as two people could be barring physical intimacy. "You know my door is always open."

"Well, I had hoped so," she admitted with a laugh. "I brought someone for you to meet."

She looked toward the floor behind them, and Ryan noticed the baby carrier for the first time. Something twisted inside of him at the sight of the dark-haired infant. Katlyn's life hadn't been easy and she deserved happiness. She and Jared were deeply in love, but her marriage had left a big void in his life.

"So this is the new little guy, huh?"

"We named him Daniel, after my dad," she explained, reaching into the carrier and lifting the tiny bundle. She cradled the baby in her arms so that he could get a better look. "This is the first time I've brought him out of the house."

Ryan studied the baby's miniature features—dark eyes, a pug nose and puckered mouth. He didn't have any experience with babies except for the animal sort, so he had no way of knowing if this one was normal and healthy.

"Is he okay? He looks awful tiny."

"You wouldn't say that if you were the one who had to deliver him," she admonished. "He weighed more than nine pounds and was twenty-one inches long."

"Is that good?"

Katlyn let out an exaggerated sigh and looked past him. "Men!" she said. "What do they know?"

He recognized the woman-to-woman tone and suddenly remembered Erica. Embarrassed at forgetting her, he felt heat ride up his neck. The apologetic smile he shot her was met with cool disdain. Ouch. He'd have to pay big-time for that mistake.

She stared directly at him, her expression aloof and unforgiving. The haughty attitude rankled. It made him want to haul her into his arms until she softened again.

"This is Katlyn King, a friend and neighbor. Katlyn, Erica Smyth. She's been helping me since I broke my arm."

The women exchanged greetings and seemed to be sizing each other up in typically female fashion.

"I met your Aunt Trudy when she brought food out to Ryan," offered Erica. "She seems like a really nice lady, and we enjoyed every bite."

"All the neighbors have pitched in to help," he added. "I've been amazed."

"You shouldn't be," said Katlyn, "You're always the first to help others. Now it's payback time. Just accept it and enjoy the attention for a while."

The heat had been receding in his neck, but Ryan felt it warm again. He'd never been comfortable accepting praise.

"Some of his friends have been especially attentive," said Erica with one of those you-know-what-I-mean looks that were invented to make men squirm. "One little Energizer bunny keeps coming back again and again. Her name's Betty Lou or Mindi Sue or something like that."

Ryan groaned, and Katlyn grinned. "Mary Jo? She's always had a thing for him."

Erica looked right at him and lifted a brow. "Yes, I can see where he might have had a thing for her, too."

He didn't want them comparing notes about his breast fetish or discussing the buxom Mary Jo. He returned Erica's steady gaze until her attention finally shifted. Then she surprised him by asking if she could hold the baby.

"Sure," said Katlyn, easing her tiny son into Erica's arms. "I'm afraid he's been a little fussy this morning, so I hope he doesn't throw a fit or spit up all over you."

"No problem," she assured her, lifting the baby to her shoulder like a seasoned pro. "I'm washable."

Erica handled him with more ease and confidence than Katlyn had shown. The baby's miniature head settled on her shoulder, his small body snuggling naturally against the curves of hers. She murmured softly to him in a soothing tone.

The image of Erica cuddling the baby knocked the breath from Ryan. A deep, unexpected hunger expanded inside of him, uncoiling so rapidly that his chest went tight with emotion. He could hardly force air in and out of his lungs. It took a minute to recover his composure.

"You're obviously used to babies. Do you have children of your own?" asked Katlyn.

"No, I'm not married. I'm just the doting aunt of two of the world's most perfect toddlers. I spend as much time with them as my schedule allows."

"You're lucky. I didn't have any practice before Daniel was born, so I'm learning by trial and error. Sometimes I panic when I realize that he's utterly dependent on me."

"My sister felt the same way, but she got the hang of it soon enough. I imagine all new mothers get a little panicked in the beginning. Children are an awesome responsibility."

"They certainly are."

The baby began to fuss, and Erica rocked him back and forth, whispering softly to quiet him.

"Do you want me to take him?" asked Katlyn.

"I think maybe he just wants a little action," said Erica. "I could take him for a walk while the two of you visit."

At Katlyn's nod, she turned toward the hall. Ryan watched her leave, his gut clenched at the sight of her cuddling the baby. It was too damned appealing. He'd never been one to hanker for offspring so the sudden, intense yearning hit him hard.

Katlyn's soft laughter brought him out of his reverie. "I think you've got it bad, my friend."

Ryan gave her a blank look, which caused her to erupt in another fit of laughter.

"What's that supposed to mean?" he asked.

"It means that you're looking at Erica like I've never seen you look at any other woman." Her eyes danced with mischief. "And I've seen you look at plenty."

"Like what?" he demanded.

"It's hard to explain."

He crossed his arms over his chest and glared. "Try."

Her expression grew thoughtful. "Kind of like a hungry male searching for a mate, a little predatory and a little possessive."

Her description hit a sensitive chord. "More than a little stupid if you think I've got permanence in mind. Erica's due to leave next week."

"Where's she going?"

"Home to Chicago. She's got a company to run."

That gave Katlyn pause, and Ryan knew she was reevaluating the information she'd learned through gossip. He didn't like to think about all the speculation on his personal life.

"She's a businesswoman?"

"Yeah, and thrives on the corporate challenge. She just took a leave of absence to work through some problems."

"It must be a very successful company if her clothing is anything to go by. That little silk number she's wearing probably cost more than I spend on clothes in a year."

The remark eased some of Ryan's tension. Katlyn admired women who worked hard and succeeded in the business world. Erica deserved the respect. He felt both relieved at his old friend's attitude and amused by her comment about the silk.

"That's her laundry outfit."

"What? I don't follow."

"She wears the silk when everything else is dirty."

Katlyn gave him a strange look. "Well, I'd bet money it has a classy designer label, so she must have a good income."

"She's an executive in her family's business, and she's damned good at it. I suppose she draws a good salary."

"Do you know her family?"

"I've never had dealings with them, but I'm doing some research on the firm. They have a good reputation, great assets and solid capital."

As they talked, Ryan ushered her into the living room where they took a seat and continued their conversation.

"How can you be so sure she's good at her job?"

"For one thing, the company's profits have increased by twenty percent each year since she joined the executive staff.

For another thing, I devised a little game that we play. I supply hypothetical problems, and she provides solutions. She's a natural. One of the best I've ever pitted my skills against."

Katlyn whistled softly. "Wow. That's high praise. You've always been a whiz at financial management. If she can impress a number-crunching genius, then she must be good."

"She's good," said Ryan, crossing one leg over the other and resting his cast on his knee. "She's been a big help with the ranch finances. I can't function too well with this cast, especially not on the computer keyboard. All I have to do is explain what I want, and she can handle it."

Katlyn commiserated about the temporary handicap, then asked, "Have you told her about Joel and the family business?"

"No. She thinks I'm a lowly cowpoke who manages a ranch. That's all that's really important."

She frowned. "Isn't that a bit deceptive? Aren't you afraid she'll be furious when she learns the truth?"

"Why should she be?"

She gave him the same look she'd been scolding him with most his life. "Ryan, your family's business is a big part of your life, even if you live and work here. She's bound to have heard of Ryersons if she's involved in the corporate world."

He and Joel were the fourth generation to run the family firm, but he only helped when they needed complicated financial analyses on specific transactions. He wanted no part of the daily business dealings, and he'd never wanted to be judged by his family's standards. That's why he hadn't mentioned the connection to Erica.

"Our relationship is based on who we are, not on corporate power, wealth or social status. There's nothing dishonest about it, and no reason for her to be upset."

"So, are you going to ask her to stay?"

His brows creased in a frown. The question had been nagging him for days, but he wasn't any closer to an answer. He pretended it didn't matter. "Why would I do that?"

She shook her head in exasperation. "It's obvious you're crazy about her. Aren't you even going to consider a more permanent relationship?"

He stared hard at her for a few seconds, and then slowly answered. "You're the only woman I ever wanted a permanent relationship with. Your marriage changed things, but it doesn't change how I feel."

After a brief pause, Katlyn responded. "You've stuck with that stubborn notion for a lot of years to avoid commitment. But this time it might not be enough."

Ryan's features tightened with annoyance. "Yeah, and now's when you tell me that what I've always felt for you is brotherly love, right?"

"It's true, whether you accept it or not. I've always been your safety net. By clinging to me, you've created an emotional buffer between you and any woman with designs on a future. It's time to quit hiding from commitment, my friend."

"And you think Erica's the woman to make the difference?"

"I don't know. Only you can be sure, but I do know you never looked at me the way you look at her. Like you want to wrap her up and hang on for dear life. The way Jared looks at me. It's a forever kind of look, and it's a whole lot different than the love we've always shared."

Ryan couldn't fault her sincerity. She'd always been open and honest with him. Maybe she was right, but he sure didn't like the picture she painted of him as an emotional coward.

"If all I ever did was use you as a buffer, that'd make me a damned shallow person, wouldn't it?"

She considered the question, and then answered carefully. "Not shallow, just wary. It's natural to be cautious about giving your heart to someone, and your family background has made you cynical. It's a big emotional risk, but it offers an even bigger payoff if you give your love to the right person."

They stared at each other for a quiet minute, two special friends coming to an understanding. Ryan knew she was right. It had taken him a long time to face the facts, but now they were staring him in the face. What he felt for her was familiar and safe. It couldn't compare with the challenge and excitement of his relationship with Erica.

Instead of the sense of loss he'd expected, he felt closure coupled with deep contentment. He and Katlyn would always share precious memories, but it was time to look toward the future.

Erica was his future.

* * * * *

At lunch the next day, Ryan asked Erica if she'd help him with some chores.

"There's not much to do in here. How can I help outside?"

"Zack and the rest of the crew will all be working cattle today. The hay in the southwest field needs to be turned, but I can't do it alone."

"You need me to rake hay?" she asked, picturing herself in a huge field with a yard rake.

He grinned. "Not exactly. We have equipment to turn hay, but it's pulled by a tractor. I need help shifting the gears."

She pursed her lips and pretended to consider the request. "So we'd both be driving a tractor?"

"Yep, and it's state of the art. Has an air-conditioned cab to protect you from too much sun. Even has a radio with a CD player."

He had that gleam in his eyes that always made her wary. "Wow, I'm impressed, but doesn't it only have one seat?"

"A nice, cushy one," he explained.

The provocative gleam in his eyes kicked her pulse into overdrive. They'd made love last night, but she could tell he wanted her again. She'd never met such a sensualist, nor thought she would want to. How wrong she'd been. His virility and stamina thrilled her, as well as his talent for creativity.

"So it's just you and me sharing a cushy seat in an air-conditioned cab. Sounds hedonistic."

His smile was roguish. "That's exactly what I thought."

The cushy seat on the tractor turned out to be Ryan's lap. He had the air conditioner running and music playing by the time she joined him. The cab wasn't very large, so they were cocooned in a big glass bubble. The tractor had eight forward gears and three gears for reverse. It was a challenge to control, but she got a kick out of learning.

The field was a long, narrow one, and they moved at a snail's pace. The equipment they were pulling looked like a giant tangle of wire hoops. It lifted and turned the hay, stirring up a sweet aroma that Ryan described as alfalfa.

Once they started, there wasn't much to do but sit, steer and enjoy the blue sky and sunshine. Ryan worked the gas pedal and steered with his good arm. He rested his cast on her lap, and they enjoyed a peaceful ride for a while. Then she asked if she could try steering, and he turned the wheel over to her.

The mistake, she belatedly realized, was freeing his hands. They settled on her bare thighs, just below her shorts, and her flesh came alive at his touch. His fingers began a slow caress that sent her blood pulsing madly through her veins.

It was always the same. He touched her, and her body throbbed to life. No matter where they were or what they were doing, the need didn't abate. It was awesome and a little frightening. She'd become addicted to his touch and didn't look forward to withdrawal.

He buried his face against the curve of her neck and nuzzled gently while his hands caressed her thighs. "Did I ever tell you I had a thing for thighs?" he murmured.

Erica sighed with pleasure, tilting her head to give him better access to the sensitive flesh.

"I think you have a 'thing' for women in general. Not just breasts and thighs."

He nudged the neckline of her shirt aside and nibbled on her shoulder. "I do have a fondness for the feminine body."

His words gave her pause. He was serious. He was an experienced lover, so did that mean he loved anyone who cared enough to share her body? Would any female do? What if she wasn't any more important to him than the others?

What about his heart? Did it belong to Katlyn? She'd overheard part of his conversation with her. He'd said she was the only woman he'd ever wanted a commitment with. Was that still true? She hadn't waited to hear Katlyn's response. Eavesdropping could prove hazardous, and she didn't want to risk a major misunderstanding.

He hadn't mentioned commitment, especially not long-term. She hadn't either, but she was old-fashioned enough to think the suggestion should come from him first.

He hadn't asked her to prolong her stay, nor suggested they had a future beyond next week. He seemed perfectly content to enjoy their time together and let her leave without a qualm.

At first the situation had seemed ideal. She'd believed an affair without commitment would be perfect. Somewhere along the way, she'd changed her mind. A permanent commitment might not be the best, but she certainly didn't want a complete break.

Ryan's fingers had slipped beneath her shorts and were slowly inching toward the juncture of her thighs. Erica's stomach muscles contracted and she gripped the steering wheel tighter. His teeth and tongue sent goose bumps dancing over her skin. It took all her concentration to keep steering.

Ryan knew just how to touch her and caress her to drive her to distraction. She would miss him abominably. Torn between her desire to get back to the company and her dread of leaving him, her heart ached whenever she thought about her departure.

"Ever had any desire to make love on a tractor?" he asked as his hot mouth seared her neck with soft, sucking kisses.

She could feel his erection pressing against her bottom and couldn't resist rocking against it. His low groan fulfilled a deep, primitive need. She wanted to excite him as much as he did her. There was no doubt that he wanted her, at least physically, and her ability to shake his composure gave her tremendous satisfaction.

"We can't make love out here," she argued.

To counter the argument, Ryan cupped a hand between her thighs and began to stroke her.

"Ryan!" She meant to scold him, but his name slipped from her lips on a gasp of pleasure.

"We're a long way from the house, and all the men are on the other side of the ranch. We have plenty of privacy."

He kept his left hand between her legs while lifting his right hand to stroke her breasts. Even though the movement of his fingers was limited, he managed to caress first one and then the other with just his fingertips. His mouth was hot on her neck and the combined caresses sent a jolt of electricity shimmering through her body.

She quivered in need.

The muscles of Ryan's thighs rippled beneath her as he braked the tractor at the end of the field. Acres of cropland spread in panoramic view around them. The afternoon sun blazed down on the tractor, but that wasn't the main source of heat. Ryan was the flame igniting her to a fever pitch of desire.

"We're supposed to be turning the hay."

"I want to make love."

The bold edict caused another shudder to race through Erica. She put the gearshift into park and turned in his arms, straddling his legs. "Right here, right now?" she asked, tossing his hat aside and running her fingers through his hair.

Ryan's voice was tight with need. "Right here, right now." He gripped her hips and held her firmly while rocking against her in masculine demand.

She loved his face, every single masculine feature. So she scattered kisses over each one, working her way to his mouth.

Ryan tugged on her shorts, and she slipped off his lap long enough to help him shove them down her legs.

"The top, too," he insisted gruffly. "I want you naked."

The fire in his eyes convinced her to acquiesce. After a brief glance all around them, she tugged off her T-shirt and bra.

He made a low, gruff sound of pleasure and pulled her back onto his lap. His mouth found hers in a deep, driving kiss that had them straining to get closer.

"You're a little overdressed, cowboy," she insisted when their mouths finally parted.

"Help me," he coaxed.

Erica slid her hands under his shirt and lifted it over his head. After tossing it to the growing pile of clothes, she stroked his chest with both hands. Crisp curls covered solid muscle and supple skin. She never got tired of touching him.

His callused fingers were gentle as they stroked her back. They kissed again, hungrily, while her hands strayed to the snap of his jeans. Taut stomach muscles quivered as she spread the fabric and reached inside to free him. Her caresses grew bolder as she sheathed him with a condom.

His low, ragged moan fueled the fire in her to a white-hot blaze. Opening herself to him, she took him deep inside. The fierce, restless hunger in him gave her a wild thrill of feminine power. This is what she'd craved all her life, the intimacy and sharing that had always been so elusive.

Ryan made her whole. He filled her body and her heart. He owned a part of her soul she hadn't known was missing. As their movements grew stronger and faster, taking them on a wild ride, she wondered how she'd ever existed without him.

How would she survive their parting?

Chapter Eleven

On Thursday, Ryan finally asked the question they'd both been avoiding. "So, what are your plans for leaving?"

Snug in the cradle of his arms, Erica went still. They'd just made love so slow and sweet and intense that she'd treasure the memory forever. Their physical bond was a perfect complement to the emotional one. He'd stolen her heart. This was the first time he'd mentioned their parting.

"Are you going to fly or drive? When do you have to go?"

"I'm due back at work on Monday, so I'll need to leave by Saturday morning," she told him in a whisper-soft voice. Emotion clogged her throat, preventing her from saying anything else until she'd regained control.

"Will said he'd like to have your used car if you're not keeping it. He's got a granddaughter who's just learning to drive, and it would be a good starter car for her."

Ryan's voice held a low, caressing tone that made the mundane sound like a melody. The timbre was seared on her memory, too.

"He's welcome to it if he wants to follow me to Iowa."

"You're driving to Iowa? What then?"

"That's where I stored my own car. I'll pick it up, spend the night there and drive on through to Chicago on Sunday."

"He might be willing to make the trip, but he wouldn't accept that kind of gift. He'd want to pay something."

"I couldn't charge him." Will and the others had become extended family. She knew how hard they worked and didn't want their money. It pleased her to be able to give something back.

"If he wants to go with me, I'd be happy to have someone share the driving. I'll need to have it transferred out of my name, too. Do you think he'd exchange services for the car?"

Her offer pleased him. She could tell by the smile in his voice. "I think that might just be a perfect solution, Red."

"You know," she forced a conversational tone. "I used to box my cousin's ears if he called me Red. He's older than I am, but I'm meaner, and he wasn't allowed to retaliate."

Ryan turned her in his arms until she lay beneath him. He leaned over her, bracing his arms on either side of her head. Solid masculine thighs slid over slim feminine ones in a sensuous glide of bare skin. The moon shone through the bedroom window, casting them in shadowy light.

"You're pretty tough, huh?" His voice dropped to a low, seductive whisper.

"Downright dangerous." She stroked his chin with her fingertips, absorbing the texture of his skin into herself.

When their gazes locked, she searched his eyes, trying to assess his true feelings. She wanted to see his soul. She was hopelessly, deathlessly in love with this man. In love for the first time in her life and terrified he didn't feel the same.

His eyes were beautiful pools of emotion. She wanted to believe he cared as deeply as she did, but she didn't trust her own instincts. Her family's wealth had left her vulnerable to men in the past. She'd lost faith in her own judgment.

"I shouldn't call you Red? You might have to hurt me."

Erica cupped his face in her hands, stroking the strong lines of his jaw with her thumbs. She needed to know if he was interested in a long-term commitment.

"I could make an exception. For a price."

"A price?" He played along with her lover's game while tangling his fingers in the tight curls of her hair.

"A reasonable price," she bargained.

"How reasonable?"

"Well, I think you'll have to pay me a kiss for every time you use the nickname."

"Hmm..." He dropped a butterfly kiss on her lips. "Is this charge retroactive? Do I have to pay for all the other nicknames I've called you?"

"Absolutely."

"Then I owe you lots of kisses, don't I?"

"It's a serious debt," she whispered huskily.

Even as he set about paying his debt, Erica's heart ached. He wasn't going to ask her to stay. He'd never mentioned seeing her again or his own connection with the corporate world. It hurt that she meant so little to him and that he could let her go so easily.

She promised herself not to get all weepy and clinging, even though, for the first time in her life, she felt like doing both. The feelings were totally alien, and she didn't know how to deal with them.

It was imperative that she go home. She'd been gone too long, and the company had always been her number one priority. She couldn't stay in Wyoming if he asked, but she perversely wanted him acknowledge that they'd reached a new level in their relationship. What a mess.

* * * * *

At eight o'clock on Saturday morning, Erica carried her belongings to the car. She'd cleaned every trace of her stay from the house, said good-bye to the staff and hugged the puppies one last time.

Will had agreed to drive her to Iowa. He would take the used car off her hands and handle the transfer of tags and title. It would save her a lot of time, plus she'd have company for part of the long trip home.

They would drive straight through to Iowa today because he wanted to get back to the ranch by early tomorrow morning. She'd stay overnight in a motel and make the last leg of the trip on Sunday. The agreement suited them both, and they'd decided to leave around nine o'clock. She'd already packed and said her goodbyes to everyone except Ryan.

After stowing the last bag, she slammed the trunk and dusted off her hands. She'd hoped to spend the morning with him, but he'd been called to a neighboring ranch before dawn. Now she didn't know if he'd even be back before she had to leave. His neglect annoyed her more with each passing minute. She felt torn between tracking him down and just leaving without a word.

The rumbling roar of a truck engine had her turning toward the sound, watching as Ryan's big pickup truck came racing toward her. As he neared, he slowed to a roll, shut off the engine and jumped out the door before the truck had completely stopped. His obvious impatience to see her improved her mood considerably.

"Hey, Red, you weren't planning to leave without a good-bye, were you?" he demanded, frowning, and searching her face with troubled eyes.

As always, the sight of him made her pulse hum. When his gaze locked with hers, she tried to appear indifferent. "We're not leaving for another hour, and you're the one who did a disappearing act."

Ryan moved closer and slid both arms around her waist, drawing her tight against his hard body. "I'm sorry, it was unavoidable. How can I possibly make it up to you?"

She slipped her arms around his neck, rolled her hips against his, and gave him a siren's smile. "I don't know, but I still have an hour before Will gets here, and I'm open to suggestions."

"In the old west, when a fellow did something bad, his dad would take him out to the woodshed."

"Really?" she asked, intrigued by the sexual gleam in his eyes as well as his train of thought. "Do you have a woodshed?"

In answer, he bent and scooped her into her arms. Erica squealed with laughter and clung to him as he strode around the back of the house. Sure enough, there was a tiny shed filled with logs for the fireplace. Ryan carried her inside and closed the door with his booted foot.

"Now what?" she asked, pressing kisses along the strong column of his throat. She felt a tremor course over his body as she sucked on his neck.

"Now you should take a belt to me or something," he murmured against her ear.

"Did you say, take your belt off?" she whispered. He eased his grip on her and she slid slowly down his body. One hand went to his belt buckle while the other stroked the hardening evidence of his arousal.

Ryan moaned, bucking his hips and rubbing himself against her palm. "Damn, but I'm going to miss you, city girl."

Erica lifted her face to his kiss, a hard, demanding kiss that stole her breath and made her heart race with excitement. His good hand slipped beneath her T-shirt, palming her left breast. When he flicked his thumb over the tightening nipple, her breathing grew ragged.

"I want you," she told him, suddenly desperate for some evidence of his caring. "Now!"

"Then help me," his lips pressed the demand to her mouth.

Erica didn't hesitate. She unfastened and unzipped his jeans and then her own. Ryan shoved some tools off a small utility counter and lifted her onto it. She took care of protection, and then he was plunging into her, filling her with his heat and hardness, making her whole.

They swallowed each other's cries of joy at the intimate joining of bodies. They fit together perfectly, moving in unison and heightening their pleasure beyond description.

She gave him her heart and soul along with her body, but she didn't have the courage to say the words. Instead, she urged him to make love to her faster and harder, showing him the emotion she couldn't verbalize. When they reached a shattering release, she cried out his name and clung to him fiercely, wondering if this would be the last time she would know such utter satisfaction.

Ryan held her close, murmuring sweetly to her until they'd both had time to recover. Then he raised his head, looking at her with those gorgeous eyes, and smiled. His smile reached deep into her soul and she knew she'd treasure the time with him more than anything else in her life.

"Consider yourself punished," she said when she could find her voice. She had to keep it light or she'd fall apart and make a total fool of herself.

"I'll take that kind of punishment anytime, sweetheart."

His statement brought a sudden change to their moods. They both knew there might not be any more times.

"I've been worried sick about leaving." There, she'd said the words aloud.

His eyes darkened as he looked into hers. "I didn't realize you had doubts. You haven't said anything, so I figured you were anxious to get back to the city."

She stared into his beautiful eyes, wondering if she could make him understand how torn she felt. “I have personal and business obligations. I’ve never been away from work this long. There’s so much to do, and I can’t keep shirking my responsibilities.”

“Your real passion?” he asked. Using just the fingertips of his broken hand, he gently stroked her cheek. “Wheeling and dealing at the corporate level?”

He’d wiped all expression from his features, so she couldn’t guess at his true feelings. Did he consider her a shallow person for caring so much about the corporate world? For caring about her reputation?

She had commitments to honor. Surely he could understand that. Did he think she should give up her life’s work for an affair with him? He’d never mentioned anything more permanent, so why would she even consider it?

“I won’t apologize for being passionate about my career. Passion is a great motivator.”

They were quiet for a long minute as they gazed into each other’s eyes. “Have you ever thought maybe you’re so passionate about the corporate world because you’ve never looked beyond it?” asked Ryan.

He brushed a thumb over her lips in a seductive caress and continued, “Maybe the executive life is your whole world because you’ve never allowed yourself to focus on anything else.”

Erica frowned, searching his face. She didn’t understand what he was getting at. “You think my vision of life is too insular?” She didn’t hear him offering alternatives.

“I’m not sure what your vision includes,” he said after a long pause, “but I want you to know you’re welcome to come back to the ranch if you ever get fed up with the business world.”

Welcome like Katlyn or Mary Jo or Trudy? Ryan's door was always open to friends and neighbors. Is that all he meant? He wouldn't turn her away if she wanted to come back? Or was he saying he'd welcome a continuation of their affair as long as no strings were attached?

Her questions went unvoiced because she couldn't work up the nerve to ask them. He hadn't offered words of love, so she didn't have much hope that he'd fallen as deeply in love with her as she had with him.

* * * * *

Erica received a warm welcome home from her parents, friends and the company staff. Everyone scolded her for the abrupt departure and for staying away so long. They wanted to know where she'd been and what she'd done, but she didn't satisfy their curiosity. She didn't feel like sharing.

Within a couple days, she'd slipped back into her normal routine without a hitch, except for the changes within herself. Wearing panty hose, high heels and power suits for twelve hours a day seemed more unpleasant than she remembered. So were the constrictive hairstyles to control her riotous curls. Makeup and jewelry seemed a nuisance, as well.

After the endless blue skies and clean, fresh air of Wyoming, the heat, humidity and smog of the city bothered her as never before. In the past, she'd taken crowded elevators, congested thoroughfares and traffic jams in stride, but now all of it grated on her nerves.

She missed Ryan, his smile, his teasing, the challenge and joy of sharing everything with him. They exchanged stilted emails, yet it didn't soothe the ache of separation.

As promised, she'd called him as soon as she got home. He hadn't been available, so she'd left a message. He'd returned her call, missed her and left a message. They'd played phone tag for days until they'd finally scheduled an exact time to call each other. The process didn't bode well for keeping in touch.

Instead of soothing her restlessness, their conversation left her frustrated and depressed. He said she sounded different, that her "Chicago voice" was detached and impersonal. She didn't explain that her tone had nothing to do with location and everything to do with missing him.

"So how are things at the office?" he'd asked. "Have you resolved your problems with the other executives? Did your dad side with them or did they come around to your way of thinking?"

Erica's lungs constricted. This was dangerous territory, possibly ruinous to their relationship. A veritable ticking bomb that she'd ignored too long. If she wasn't careful, the Ryerson deal could destroy everything between them. She fought to sound cool and collected.

"You won't believe this, but they totally scratched the plans that had me so worried. And it had nothing to do with my concerns," she said with a sigh. "It seems we got a better offer while I was gone, so now they've switched gears entirely."

When she thought about the weeks of wasted anger and frustration it made her wonder at the insanity of it all. She couldn't regret it, though. It had led her to Ryan.

"So what do you think about the new offer?"

This she could answer without hesitation. "I'm thrilled with it. The merger will give us everything Steven wants in the international scope and allow us to maintain our status quo with our smaller, less productive companies. The prospect of a merger is causing a stir in our little corporate community, too, and increasing the value of our stock."

"You're sure the deal is good for your firm?"

"Absolutely. Steven's taking credit for the whole thing and has assured us that all the terms are favorable. I've been checking the fine print in case there's some underlying threat to our business, but I haven't found anything that puts us at risk. Only incredible benefits."

Ryan went quiet for a minute, and then asked, "Are you ticked because Steven's getting all the credit?"

Erica laughed softly. Two months ago, she might have been green with envy, but not so much now. Something very elemental in her makeup seemed to have shifted. Maybe Ryan was right about her drive stemming from so little knowledge of any other life.

"Surprisingly, no. We've always been competitive, but I don't begrudge him a success that benefits everyone."

"Fortune 500 company?"

"Ryersons," she said, holding her breath and hoping against hope that he'd reveal his connection to the Ryerson empire. He had to be behind the generous terms they'd been offered. There were so many questions she wanted answered. She wanted to thank him and share her enthusiasm, but first he had to trust her with the truth.

"So when do you finalize the deal?"

"In a couple weeks or so. I don't think we have a date set yet." His question gave her the lead-in she needed to ask, "So when are you going to come see me?"

He seemed startled by the suggestion. He hedged and she felt the sharp sting of disillusionment. Was the Ryerson deal his idea of a thank-you for great sex? Did he consider it his parting gift to her? Her throat tightened.

"Chicago's a long way from the ranch. I don't have that kind of time right now."

"You could fly out for a weekend visit," she suggested. It was as close to begging as her pride would allow. Even though he couldn't see her, warmth crept into her cheeks.

The heat of embarrassment increased when he went quiet for several seconds. Maybe he didn't want to come, or maybe he couldn't afford it. She had no way of knowing his personal finances. His family was wealthy, but maybe he lived on a manager's income. She'd gladly pay his way, yet she wouldn't bruise his pride by offering.

"It sounds real nice, Red." His voice finally took on a low, seductive pitch that shimmied through the phone lines and straight to her heart. "I just don't know how soon I can make it. I've got a cattle buying trip next week, and then it might take another week to settle a financial matter for the guy who owns the ranch."

Erica wanted to argue, to demand they make time for each other, but pride kept her from saying any more on the subject. She tried to accept his gentle rejection, and hid her disappointment during the rest of their conversation. He didn't invite her to fly to Wyoming, and she didn't suggest it. For all she knew, he'd already found someone else to warm his bed.

A part of her believed he cared deeply, but another, more persistent part, doubted her ability to inspire undying love and devotion in any man. Ryan was warm and good-hearted and down-to-earth in his home on the range. She was cool, reserved and thrived in the insular world of high finance and high society. Maybe they just weren't meant to be together.

Their calls over the next couple weeks were sporadic and brief. Erica knew it would be best to make a clean break, but she couldn't bring herself to stop communicating with him altogether. After particularly hectic days, the sound of his voice soothed her as nothing else could do.

Nearly three weeks after her return to Chicago, Smyth-Kessler held a formal reception and dinner for the executives of Ryersons. It would be her first opportunity to meet the men behind the conglomerate with which Smyth-Kessler would merge.

More than a hundred associates were gathered in a hotel banquet room the company had rented for the event. A small band played quietly in one corner while waiters circulated with champagne and hors d'oeuvres. Tables were prepared for elegant dining, and everyone was dressed in their finest with hopes of making a good impression.

Erica wore a shimmering, full-length gown of peacock blue. The soft, clinging fabric of its bodice draped over her right shoulder in Grecian style and left the other one bare. A starburst of rainbow-colored sequin threads started at one shoulder and splayed to her opposite hip.

High-heeled silver sandals and long, silk-covered legs peeked from beneath two deep slits in the slim-fitting skirt. Her hair had been tamed into a neat chignon with just a few stray curls.

Erica and a few friends stood chatting while they awaited the guests of honor. As usual, the women were good-naturedly dissecting the appearance of the men in the room.

"Mark Peterson sure looks different in formalwear, doesn't he? I wonder if he's involved with anyone?" Ellen had recently divorced and was considering a replacement for her ex.

"I think the new guy, Briggs, from accounting, has possibilities. Remind me to ask him for a dance," said Sharon.

"Tom Sands shouldn't wear black. He's so pale, it makes him look like a corpse." Steven's secretary had a thing for Tom, but they were both too timid to do anything about it.

"I never realized Jack Minnon had such nice buns," put in Donna, the firm's receptionist and resident manhunter.

That brought a collective chuckle and reminded Erica of Ryan. Nearly everything reminded her of him. The last time they'd talked, he'd ended their conversation by saying, "I'll see you soon". Then he'd abruptly hung up without explaining. She'd been fantasizing about seeing him, and spent altogether too much time thinking about him. She shouldn't waste the time and was annoyed with herself for being so easily distracted.

"Heads up," said Sharon. "I think our VIPs have arrived."

All eyes turned toward the double doors near the center of the room. Three well-dressed men paused at the top of a small staircase. Erica watched her dad and cousin separate from a group of friends and approach them. The visitors descended the stairs and offered their hands in welcome.

"Wow, that dark-haired one must be the big guy, Joel Ryerson. I heard he was a hunk," said Ellen. "The other two look too old to fit his profile."

Erica studied the man in question, agreeing that he fit all the descriptions she'd read of Ryerson. Tall and lean, his dark hair was cut conservatively short. Although not storybook handsome, he had an air of assurance that reeked sex appeal.

"Maybe you should go over there and check him out," Sharon urged her. "I've heard he's single and available. You could talk all sorts of mergers with him."

Erica smiled, knowing she really should go and greet their guests, yet she felt strangely hesitant. Then another man stepped through the doors and captured her attention. His calm, confident demeanor staggered her breathing.

Ryan. Her Ryan. Her heart.

Dressed in a western-cut tux, he looked tall, broad-shouldered and utterly gorgeous. The sight of him stirred the curiosity of every woman in the room. She heard collective murmurs of interest from her friends, but then the sound of her pulse drumming in her ears deafened her to their voices.

He slowly surveyed the room until his gaze fastened on her. When their eyes met, he smiled, a slower-than-molasses smile so wide and sexy that it filled her with incredible joy. The special, intimate smile of greeting warmed her body from head to toe and everywhere between.

Weeks of worrying and wondering became insignificant. A chorus of inquiries rose from her friends, but Erica didn't respond. She didn't question his unexpected appearance, she just knew she had to get to him, to touch him and let his presence fill the emptiness that gnawed at her.

There was no hesitancy in her steps as she crossed the room in a slow, elegant glide of silk and sequins. Drawn to Ryan by an invisible bond, she never lost eye contact and her steps never faltered. A sea of bodies parted as she gracefully made her way to him.

He slowly descended the steps and reached out to her the instant they were close enough to touch. She gave him her hand, and he lifted it to his lips, pressing a kiss on it that sent ribbons of excitement up her arm. The expression on his face told her he wanted so much more.

"Hi, cowboy," she managed in a tight whisper. Her heart pounded with excitement, the throb of her pulse drowning out everything but him.

"Hi, city girl." His voice sounded like music, his tone a seductive treat.

He reached for her other hand and brought both to his lips again, pressing a long, slow kiss on each. Her nerves sizzled with such a thrill that she trembled. His touch made her feel warm and alive and whole again.

Then she noticed his cast was gone. "Your cast? You got it off. But it hasn't been a full six weeks, has it?"

"Almost. I threatened Doc. Told him if he didn't cut it off, I would."

Erica laughed softly, loving the wicked gleam in his eyes. Her heart raced as joy spread throughout her body. It was a simple, yet fabulous joy of just being near him again. Every cell of her body tingled with anticipation.

She shocked them both a little when she grasped his hand and brought it to her lips, gently kissing the pale skin where his cast had been. His eyes darkened, the teasing light altering to a predatory hunger that matched the one roaring through her.

Engrossed in each other, it took them a minute to realize they were being included in someone else's conversation. Her parents and all the executives had shifted closer to them.

"I'd like to introduce you to my brother if I can pry him away from Ms. Kessler for a minute," said a deep baritone.

Erica glanced toward Joel Ryerson. He was smiling, his gaze going from Ryan to her and back to Ryan. They'd never met in person, but he obviously recognized her.

"Brother?" she said, knowing she had to make a comment. The time of reckoning was nearing. Her pulse galloped as she tried to decide whether to play the aggrieved girlfriend or to come clean with the whole truth. She didn't want an audience when she confessed, so she continued the pretense.

Ryan tensed, his brows creasing in a frown. His grip on her hands tightened. "Joel and I are brothers. We just don't share the same last name," he explained.

Erica feigned surprise at the news. She pretended to be a little hurt and confused, but not angry. Her reaction might backfire when he learned the whole truth.

He'd once called her a chameleon. Now she returned the appellation. "I guess I'm not the only chameleon here," she said, keeping her voice light, but tugging her hands from his grip and taking a step backward.

Ryan ignored the others and gently grasped her arms, pulling her close again. "Don't be angry. I'm not some kind of changeling," he insisted. "You know the real me," he added more gruffly. "I'm just a simple man with simple needs."

Chapter Twelve

Erica looked into Ryan's beautiful, mesmerizing eyes. They spoke of love and adoration and a powerful yearning that matched her own. There was nothing simple about the man, yet she didn't doubt his commitment to the way of life he'd taught her. It stung that he'd never fully identified himself to her, but he'd never mislead her about the things he considered most important.

He'd orchestrated the merger because he'd thought that would relieve her worries. He had nothing to gain except her happiness. In true western tradition, he'd been looking after his woman. It was archaic and chauvinistic, romantic and old-fashioned and utterly endearing.

"Erica?" His fingers caressed her arms, his tone coaxing her to accept his interference. All he asked in return was for her to trust him.

And she did. Ryan was a beautiful person inside and out, a man she'd grown to love more than life. She could easily forgive him, but would he forgive her? Trust was a two-way street and she'd been equally guilty of withholding it.

She gave him a slow smile, promising herself to confess later. He closed his eyes briefly and sighed as the tension eased between them. Then he released her arms and slipped a hand behind her waist, turning toward the others.

"Maybe you'd better introduce me to your brother," she suggested lightly.

Erica suddenly noticed that everyone in the whole room was watching with undiluted curiosity and mixed expressions. Joel and his associates were smiling with satisfaction. So were her parents. Steven and Geoffrey were looking a bit stunned.

"Joel, meet Erica Kessler. She's a special friend and a corporate powerhouse," Ryan boasted, tugging her close to his side. "Erica, my brother, Joel, also a powerhouse."

The two shook hands and then Erica introduced Ryan to her mother and dad. She warned everyone to be gentle with the handshake since he'd just gotten rid of a cast. He grumbled that he wasn't an invalid, and she fussed with him for rushing his recovery. The banter continued while introductions were made.

Once everyone had met, Steven attempted to regain control of the situation and restore some decorum. He suggested they all take a seat at the banquet table.

"Actually," Ryan injected smoothly. "They're playing our song, and I'd like to have this dance with Erica."

Her brows rose in surprise, and she shot a glance at Joel. He smiled slightly, obviously accustomed to his brother playing by his own set of rules. It didn't appear to bother him. She decided she liked him on the spot.

"Excuse us," she murmured politely as Ryan guided her toward the tiny, empty dance floor.

"Our song?" she taunted. "We can't even agree on the best style of music, let alone a favorite."

"Any song that gets you in my arms is my favorite right now," he swore softly, turning her into his embrace and grasping her waist with both hands.

"How utterly uncivilized," she suggested, tilting her head back to study his beloved features.

"I've about had it with civilization," he grumbled, his tone low and rough. "I've spent the last ten days flying back and forth across the country, undergoing an intensive interrogation from my family, and battling the concrete jungle of New York. It always makes me feel uncivilized. I'm tired, frustrated and in need of some TLC." He gave her a look hot enough to make her blood sizzle.

Erica smiled in sympathy, and then slid her palms up his chest under his jacket. The cotton of his shirt was cool and stiff, but the body beneath it was warm and solid. The steady beat of his heart caused her pulse to leap with pleasure.

She gently rotated with the music until her hips and thighs were snug against his. Muscle to muscle, pulse to pulse, they began a slow glide around the floor. He closed his eyes briefly in ecstasy as she slipped her arms around his neck, pressing her breasts against his chest. A hungry male groan rumbled from deep in his chest as he tightened his hold on her.

She rested her head on his shoulder, and he nuzzled her ear. "What're the chances of blowing this joint?"

"Slim to none."

He groaned. "I'll plead a headache and jet lag, then you can take me to your apartment."

"I still live with my parents."

He muttered an oath. "Lucky thing I insisted on my own hotel room instead of sharing a suite with Joel. How soon can we get out of here without completely destroying your reputation?"

"I'll insist they hold off the business discussions until tomorrow. Mother will back me up, but we still have to eat dinner and play nice for a while."

Ryan palmed the back of her head and tilted it until she looked directly into his eyes. The heat she saw there caused a shiver of reaction.

"I can't wait that long to kiss you," he insisted gruffly. "Is there a balcony or broom closet where we can be alone?"

She gave him a siren's smile and nodded. Several other couples had joined them on the floor and someone had dimmed the lights in the area. They were no longer the center of attention, so she slowly guided him toward a nearby door. It opened onto a tiny balcony with a lovely view of the river.

As soon as they'd closed the doors behind them, Ryan clutched her close. His eyes burned with the heat of passion as his mouth dipped to hers. "I've been going crazy for the taste of you," he whispered as their lips brushed in a gentle caress.

It was as close as he'd ever come to expressing his feelings for her. The admission sent her heart soaring, but the burden of guilt on her conscience grew heavier.

"I'm a little crazy about you, too," she whispered back, her throat tightening with emotion.

"Kiss me," he commanded, locking their mouths together in a ravenous kiss. He thrust his tongue into her mouth, tasting and tantalizing and pleasing her with his urgent need. She rocked closer to him, wanting to be absorbed into his body, wanting to absorb him into hers and make them one.

The kisses were long and deep. When he finally released her, they were both trembling for more.

"Damn, I wish we didn't have to play nice with the corporate set," Ryan insisted on a ragged breath.

Her breathing was just as rough. The kisses hadn't banked fires, just added fuel to them. She tried to calm herself. "We'd better gear down a little," she teased.

"Later," he promised in a whisper near her ear as they reentered the banquet room. "How about a drink for now?"

"Sounds good," said Erica. She quickly pulled herself together and led him toward the open bar.

Steven waylaid them before they could even order a drink.

"Erica, I've got to hand it to you, you've outdone yourself this time."

She glanced nervously from one man to the other, fervently hoping Steven wouldn't say anything to divulge her secret before she could confess.

"She's amazing, isn't she?" Ryan gave her a special smile.

"Sure is." Steven's tone was a little slurred, evidence that he'd already had too much to drink. "Yes, sir, when Erica Kessler sets her sights on a man or a corporate partner, she doesn't mess around. She goes for the biggest and best."

Ryan went still and turned his full attention to Erica, leaving her no time to hide her reaction. Furious with Steven and momentarily panicked, she felt heat climbing her cheeks.

"Sets her sights?"

She couldn't look directly at Ryan. Instead, she glared at Steven. "I think you've had enough to drink. Why don't you see if our other guests need attention?" His expression smug, he gave a shrug and sauntered back toward the banquet tables.

Ryan's tone was low and dangerous. "Erica? You knew who I was all along?" When she didn't respond immediately, he added, "Just a yes or no. Did you know my connection with Ryersons?"

Anger and resentment were already rolling off him in waves. Gone was the congenial lover, in his place a big, angry male. The abrupt change was startling. She'd never experienced the brunt of his temper, so it took all her courage to look him in the eyes. "I knew before I left Wyoming."

His expression turned fierce and tight with contempt, but he didn't say a word. He just turned on his heel and headed toward the exit with long, angry strides.

Panic raced through Erica and exploded in her chest. "Ryan!" she called, racing after him. High heels and a snug-fitting gown slowed her progress. "Wait!" she insisted, grabbing her skirts and hiking them for more legroom.

He ignored her and strode from the ballroom. By the time she made it up the stairs and out of the room, the elevator door was closing behind him. She raced to another one and punched the down button. As soon as it arrived, she stepped inside, punching the close button repeatedly, impatient to catch him before he got out of the building.

By the time the elevator reached the lobby and the doors slid open, Ryan was being swallowed by revolving doors. She hiked up her skirt again and ran. He was climbing into a limousine when she hit the sidewalk in front of the hotel.

"Hold that, please!" she shouted at the bellhop closing the limo door. He paused and glanced her way, his expression wary, but she gave him what she hoped was a big, confident smile. "I decided to join him after all."

Without allowing him time to question her actions, Erica crawled into the limo and collapsed onto the seat. She fought to catch her breath, annoyed that her breathing sounded labored while Ryan sat in utter silence. It took several minutes to calm herself enough to speak.

"I deserve a chance to explain," she finally managed.

His tone was hard and uncompromising. "A waste of time."

He stared straight ahead, his attitude suggesting he couldn't care less. The only indication of pent-up emotion came from the angry loosening of his tie and collar.

Erica knew she'd done more than infuriate him. She'd hurt him and broken his faith in her. She'd hoped he would take the news without feeling betrayed, but she'd badly miscalculated. Until he'd walked into that banquet room with love and adoration shining from his eyes, she hadn't fully realized what she'd been risking with her silence.

Offense seemed the best defense. "You deliberately kept your connection to Ryersons a secret," she said. "And you expected me to accept the fact without complaining."

"Save it," he snapped. "It's not the same and you know it." He jerked the tie off his neck and shoved it in his pocket, still refusing to look at her as the limo pulled from the curb.

"I didn't say it was the same, but I promised myself I'd confess my secret as soon as you trusted me with yours."

Ryan didn't bother to respond. Her arguments weren't making a dent in his anger, but she knew they were pretty lame. She wouldn't have been appeased, either. He thought she'd manipulated him from the beginning. It'd be a blow to anyone's pride. Erica decided to change tactics.

"I'm sorry," she apologized, her voice going low and throaty. Even though she knew he deserved the apology, it wasn't easy to make. "I'm sorry I didn't tell you that I knew you were Joel Ryerson's brother."

That had his head whipping around, his eyes steely as he glared at her. "You knew from the beginning? At Bubba's?"

Erica shook her head vigorously. "No. Not at the bar."

"When?" he growled. "When did you know for sure? How long did you play your little game of pretend? How much of our relationship was built on lies?"

"I never played games with you," she insisted, flinching when he uttered a harsh oath. His bitterness hurt, but she fought to keep her tone even. "I didn't find out until I had my assistant run a background check on you."

Ryan swore again, and Erica swallowed hard. Instead of pacifying him, she just kept adding fuel to his anger.

"So you deliberately set out to seduce me."

"No!" Erica denied the accusation. "That's not true. I don't do business that way, whether you believe it or not. I've never seduced a prospective business associate, and I never asked you for anything. I am not some whore for sale to the highest bidder!"

"Then explain how the hell you ended up in my backyard. Did you plan to ingratiate yourself and then ask for favors?"

Erica's heart pounded violently in her chest, and her nerves were strung tight. She stopped twisting her hands in her lap, and tried to calm herself.

"I told you the truth about leaving Chicago. I was furious with my dad and totally fed up with the business. I wanted some time and distance to reevaluate things, but I didn't consciously decide to track you down. I remembered reading that Ryerson had a brother in Wyoming and maybe subconsciously headed in that direction, but I swear I never planned to seek you out or ingratiate myself."

"Until I was injured and needed help?" he snapped.

Erica flushed, suddenly too shy to admit she'd been infatuated with him from the very first night they'd met. "I decided to just follow your lead and see where it took us."

Ryan's low grunt didn't encourage her to expand on that particular subject. They were both quiet for a few minutes, each staring straight ahead. Then he hit the intercom button and told the driver to take them back to the hotel.

A new wave of panic surged through Erica. He wanted to be rid of her. It hurt so much that her lungs constricted. Her hands trembled. She didn't know what to say in her own defense.

"Don't worry," Ryan told her brusquely. "I'm not going to interfere with the Ryerson-Kessler deal. I'll leave the wheeling and dealing to you and Joel. I'm fed up with the whole mess. You can go back to the party and suck up to him for a while. If you play your cards right, you could end up in his bed tonight."

The cruelty of his words spurred her anger and gave strength to her voice. She turned more fully toward him. "I don't give a damn about your brother or the deal."

His bitter, disbelieving laughter prompted her to narrow the distance between them. Close enough that she could feel the tension gripping him. He cared. She had to believe that. She couldn't give up on their relationship without being totally honest, without sharing some of what was in her heart.

"I know you don't want to believe me, but all I can do is swear I'm telling the truth. I'll always want what's best for Kessler's, but I'm more concerned about you and me."

"There is no you and me," he ground out roughly. "You wanted a merger, and you got it. We had an affair, but I lost interest. End of story."

Erica hated the quiver in her voice, but not nearly as much as she hated his cold indifference. "You can't mean that."

"The hell I can't."

Closing her eyes, she searched her memory for an image. She needed a reminder of how he'd greeted her earlier this evening. He couldn't have faked the joy at seeing her, nor the hunger in his kisses. Her deception couldn't have destroyed every trace of love. There had to be a spark left to ignite. She just had to find a way to reach past his wounded pride.

They'd be back at the hotel soon, and she was running out of time. The only option left was setting aside her pride and opening her heart. It meant revealing a vulnerability she'd never shown anyone. It took all her courage, but his love was worth the risk.

Kicking off the heels, she grabbed her skirt and pulled it to her thighs. Then she slid across the seat and boldly straddled Ryan's lap. His eyes went wide with surprise, his mouth tightened and his body went rigid, but he didn't try to dislodge her.

Except for the first time she'd tried to seduce him, she'd never been very aggressive in their loving. She wasn't sure how he'd react, but the intimate contact shot a current of electricity between them. His reaction proved he wasn't as immune as he wanted to be. It encouraged her to continue.

With blood pounding loudly in her ears, Erica flattened her hands on his chest. The feel of his strong, hard body made her quiver with longing, but she resisted the urge to shift closer. She wanted his full attention, and she had it.

"I understand your anger. I deserve it." Her throat was so dry she had to swallow and lick her lips before continuing. "I should have told you the truth as soon as I realized who you were. But I didn't keep it a secret for financial or corporate gains. I kept it for me. Because I had a chance to explore an attraction that was beyond my experience. I'd found something, no," she corrected, "someone who tempted me to put my career ambitions aside for a while."

"So it's the sex that's important?" he asked coldly. "If that's what you really want, I guess I can oblige you there."

He held Erica's gaze while he hit the intercom, telling the driver to switch course again.

For the first time since crawling onto Ryan's lap, she dropped her gaze. He wanted to punish her by making her feel lower than dirt, and he'd succeeded. She hated being treated like some high-class call girl. The only alternative was to make him understand what was in her heart, but she'd never been very good at sharing her innermost feelings.

She took a deep breath, but couldn't look him in the eyes. "I can't remember ever being more than an extension of my father," she explained quietly, smoothing the cotton of his shirt with trembling fingers. The heat of his skin burned through the fabric.

"All my life, I've worked toward one goal. Filling my father's shoes. I didn't even realize how much of an executive clone I'd become until I found the courage to leave Chicago. Until I'd experienced Bubba's and worked beside you at the ranch. You helped me realize that I have a lot more to offer the world and myself than sixteen hours a day in an office tower."

Erica glanced up but couldn't hold his gaze while she bared her soul. She fiddled with the collar of his shirt. The vee of his skin tantalized her to brush a fingertip across his throat. He shuddered. She hoped with pleasure, not contempt, yet she didn't dare a glance at him.

When he didn't offer any resistance to her caress, she relaxed a little and eased herself more fully into his lap. Her skirt rode up to her waist as she sank against the growing evidence of his desire. The contact sent a quiver of longing over her. She closed her eyes and forced back a moan.

"Sex," Ryan declared roughly. "Just sex."

Instead of sounding dismissive, his tone went low and rough. His body vibrated with emotion, and Erica knew it was more than sexual tension. She had to believe he cared and cared deeply. She had to convince him that she cared as much.

Sliding her hands up his neck, she cupped his face in her palms. The anger in his eyes had been replaced by wariness and a vulnerability that matched hers. They stared at each other for a long moment. This time, Erica didn't try to hide all that she felt for him.

"I love you so much," she whispered, her voice thick with tears. "Whatever I've done or said or been in the past means nothing. I'm not the same woman who fled Chicago for Kingston. Getting to know you has changed me. All I want is you. Your love, your trust, your heart."

She watched through a mist of tears as myriad expressions chased across his face. Her confession of love blasted away his anger. He looked wary and then rigidly controlled again. He held her gaze for what seemed an eternity, but she didn't try to mask her emotions. She allowed him a peek into her soul.

When she didn't think she could stand the strain any longer, his hands slid over her thighs to settle on her waist. His touch unraveled her composure. She closed her eyes and a sob caught at her throat.

"No!" Ryan growled as she swayed closer.

Erica stiffened again as fear shot through her. She didn't know if she could stand his continued rejection. She opened her eyes, prepared to beg, but the words got trapped in her throat.

"Don't cry," he whispered gruffly, trapping a teardrop with his mouth. The feel of his lips on her face dragged another sob from her. She slid her hands into his hair and tugged until their mouths were aligned. Then she kissed him with a hunger that left no doubt about her feelings.

A low groan escaped Ryan as their tongues dueled. He wrapped his arms around her and shifted until she was as close as the confines allowed. Chest to chest, hips to hips, they strained against each other until the limo came to a stop.

Chapter Thirteen

Ryan unlocked the door of his hotel room and tugged Erica inside. He put out the "Do Not Disturb" sign, closed and locked the door, then pulled her into his arms.

"Erica," he whispered roughly as he found her mouth with his. He loved the feel of her arms as they locked around his neck and the feel of her strong, supple body pressed close. She was all woman, soft and shapely and warm. Her scent sparked a deep hunger, her taste was sweeter than wine.

While they kissed, they were busy ridding each other of clothes. He'd already stripped off his jacket. She helped get him out of his shirt and they both kicked off their shoes.

Slowly, and with great pleasure, he unzipped her dress. As the fabric peeled away and slid from her body, his breath stilled. It was the first time he'd caressed her bare skin with both hands. Her back was soft and smooth while her nipples prodded his chest like plump velvet buttons. He hugged her and buried his tongue in the honeyed sweetness of her mouth.

The feel of her sent desire cutting through him, jagged and rough. Blood pumped in a fiery riot through his veins. It pooled, hot and heavy, in his groin. When their lips finally parted, he nuzzled her neck, intoxicated by the scent of her skin. He'd missed her more than he'd thought possible, and he wanted her with a desperation that shook his control.

"The bed," he insisted gruffly, then swung her up in his arms and carried her there. He couldn't last much longer.

Setting her on the edge of the bed, he stepped between her knees and reached for the fastener holding her hair. He loved her wild curls and wanted to see them splayed against her bare shoulders.

Erica busied herself unfastening his pants, sliding them down his legs so that he could kick them aside. He combed his fingers through her hair then stroked her shoulders and breasts. He loved the eager sounds humming in her throat.

Her touch shot hot currents of need through his veins as she rid him of his briefs. Then she stroked him and he was the one who moaned in an agony of need. Knowing he was nearing the point of no return, he pressed her back against the mattress and spread her thighs with his own. He sucked one taut nipple into his mouth while stroking the other with his thumb. She whimpered, and he nearly lost it.

"Protection," he insisted.

"I'll take care of it," she whispered, nearly shattering what was left of his control in the process.

He couldn't wait any longer. He joined their bodies as gently as possible, but swiftly lost what little bit of control he'd had. Their mouths locked with the same fierce hunger that had their bodies straining. He tried to hold back, but Erica wouldn't allow it. She urged him for closer, harder, faster penetration that soon had them both spiraling out of control.

He collapsed against her until he could catch his breath and some of the strength returned to his limbs. Then he pulled the covers over them and cuddled her close.

They needed to talk.

"What now, city girl?" One shaded lamp cast her features in soft light, and he studied her intently.

"I love you," she whispered softly. "I'm not sure where we go from here, but I'm willing to explore the options."

"I've given it a lot of thought," he said, stroking her hair from her face and caressing her cheek. He just couldn't get enough of her. "I'm not involved with the day-to-day operation of Ryersons, so I handle my end of the business from the ranch. Do you think there's a chance you could divide your time between city and country?"

The warmth of her palms settled on his chest. "I've given it a lot of thought, too. There's no way I could hold my current status in the company and spend so much time out of state."

Ryan felt his heart constrict. Then she continued.

"I never thought it was possible, but I've begun to think about giving up my executive position altogether. Maybe I could work as an advisor, like you do for Ryersons."

He was almost afraid to believe what he was hearing. "You mean you wouldn't mind leaving the city on a permanent basis? You'd be happy on the ranch?" It was more than he'd dared hope.

"It hasn't been the same since I came home," she said. "Maybe you were right about my career. Maybe the corporate lifestyle suited me so well because I'd never tried anything else. I'm sure I'll still crave the adrenaline high once in a while, but life is all about adjusting to change, isn't it?"

"Ranching isn't very glamorous," he reminded.

"No, but it's real. Real people who are real friends. I've thought about how your neighbors pitched in to help out when you were hurt. If that happened in my family, our friends would be quick to send flowers or gifts. But I can't think of even one who would take the trouble to cook for us and make sure we had anything we needed. That's a sad thing to consider, and I think I prefer your world to the only other one I've ever known."

Ryan spirits soared. His lady love was considering changing lifestyles for him. "How about the excitement of the city? I thought you had a passion for the fast pace."

"Funny thing," she whispered, nibbling his chin, "without you, the pace is tedious and the lights are really dim."

"Honest?"

"Honest. And every since I came home, I've been thinking about the future, my future, our future. I'd like a family of my own sometime soon," she whispered wistfully. "I want children, and I'd like them to know the best of both our worlds."

Ryan smothered the last word with a kiss, expressing his exultation without words, telling her that he shared the dream. Her declaration of love had wiped out his anger and resentment. He didn't plan to tell Erica, but he was glad she hadn't told him the truth in the beginning. Then he would have missed knowing her and watching her blossom like a flower to the sun.

He'd make sure she never regretted her decision to trust him. She'd never want for anything as long as it was in his power to provide it. When they finally drew apart, he slipped from the bed and went to the room's safe. He returned with a small jeweler's box and presented it to her.

Erica's eyes widened and she sat up, tucking the sheet under her arms. When she opened the box, her eyes and mouth grew rounder. She stared at him in amazement.

"Will you marry me?" he asked, gazing into beautiful eyes that began to glisten with tears. "We can make it work, I swear. We'll make our home in Wyoming, but we can travel back and forth to Chicago as often as you want. I'm filthy rich, you know. I can take you anywhere you want to go. If you never want to work another day, it's up to you. If you want to open an office in Kingston, I'll help you there, too."

The smile she gave him was exquisite. It made his chest hurt and he felt like shouting with joy.

She tried to speak, had to clear her throat, and then tried again. "You are an incredibly special man," she whispered, cupping his face in her palm. "I think I'll have to marry you."

Ryan let out a triumphant yell and crawled into bed again. He gave her a long, lingering kiss, then returned their attention to the ring. "Do you like it?" he asked. He'd chosen a marquis-shaped diamond solitaire. "We can exchange it for something else."

"It's gorgeous, and I love it!" she insisted. She took the box in her hands, watching the gem flash with brilliance. "Will you put it on for me?"

He lifted the ring from its velvet nest and slipped it on her finger. Next he lifted her hand to his mouth and kissed it. The ring sparkled, but not more brightly than Erica's eyes. Her reaction made him feel humble and incredibly lucky.

"I love you, now and forever."

"That's good," she whispered huskily, pulling him along with her as she slid down in the bed, "because forever's exactly how long I plan to love you."

"Really?" He nibbled on her lips. "For better and worse?"

"Really." She teased him with her tongue. "Until death."

"Good." He caught her lips in a kiss to seal the promise.

Enjoy An Excerpt From:

HANCHART LAND

Susan decided she'd take a dip in the pool when she felt a little more rested. After applying some sunscreen, she stretched out on the lounge chair. It was really comfortable and the sun felt wonderful. She pulled the stretchy band from her hair so that she could lay her head down flat, and within minutes she was sound asleep.

Some time later that sleep brought her incredibly erotic dreams. She had the total, undivided attention of a faceless, nameless man who came for no other reason than to please her. It began with a massage by strong hands using warm, fragrant oil.

He started with her toes and then inched his way over the ball of her foot to her arch. His thumbs worked magic as they gently but firmly stroked her instep until she felt a warm tingling sensation creep up her spine.

First one foot and then the other received highly focused attention. Susan heard herself moan with pleasure as more ripples of sensual bliss bombarded her. The hands moved slowly up her calves, rubbing and caressing muscle and flesh until every nerve ending in her body was alive with seductive heat.

Her thighs were especially sensitive and the hands stroked them with a liquid heat that set her on fire. She whimpered and shifted her legs in little, restless twitches. Then the hands had her hands, caressing each ringless finger, her thumbs and palms. Her arms were molded and stroked until her toes curled and a whole new sort of tension invaded her body.

She whimpered again softly when the palms of his hands skimmed over her ribs and ever so lightly across her breasts, bringing her nipples into aching fullness with just the briefest touch.

When the callused yet tender hands kneaded her shoulders, caressed her neck and finally cupped her face, an image of a face behind the hands began to form. Susan lifted her heavy lids and looked directly into deep-set gray eyes that were watching her with such shattering intensity it stole what was left of her breath.

Luke's upper body was shading her eyes from the sun, so she had no problem seeing his face beneath the rim of his Stetson. His features were totally devoid of emotion, making it impossible to gauge his reaction to touching her so freely.

"You're going to get burned," was all he said as he took more of the lotion into his hands.

There were a lot of ways to get burned, but Susan couldn't worry about them now. She just felt—alive, aware, aroused. She tried to drag herself to alertness, but she was dazed by the blatant sensuality of his ministrations.

His hands continued to massage her cheeks, his thumbs at her temples. Then his fingers slid into her hair, combing it from her face before he moved his fingertips to massage her scalp.

She carefully studied his face as he concentrated on his self-appointed task. If he was as shaken by the contact as she was, he didn't show it.

"Turn over and I'll do your back," he commanded, his tone low but completely controlled.

Her expression told him she didn't know if she could bear any more of his erotic attentions, but he ignored the message and gently helped her turn onto her stomach.

She was wide awake now, yet the sensation of floating in a dreamlike state remained with her as his hands worked a similar magic on her shoulders, back and hips.

By the time he'd spread the sunscreen over the backs of her thighs, every nerve ending in her body was quivering with unrestrained excitement.

He grasped her hips and helped her turn so that she was facing him again. Susan felt as boneless and limp as a dishrag. She could only stare at him in mute fascination at his effortless manipulation of her senses.

Luke had been hunched down beside her, but stood to his full height and seemed especially tall from her vantage point. He was still dressed in his work clothes but his eyes were hidden from her as he looked down on her.

"Rosa suggested I bring you lemonade and remind you to put on more sunscreen," he explained.

Apparently he'd decided to take the housekeeper's suggestions to a higher level. She knew she must look like a wanton at the very least. He'd managed to thoroughly arouse her.

A glance at his jeans proved he was aroused, too, but in firm control of his desires. He obviously didn't intend to take his seduction any further, even though she just as obviously wouldn't object.

Her voice, when she tried to speak, was no more than a thready whisper. Pushing up on her elbows, she reached for the lemonade he'd placed on a nearby table. A sip of it helped clear her throat and she voiced the only coherent thought that came to mind.

"Thank you."

She was thanking him for his unselfish attentions, and for remaining in control when some men would have taken advantage of her vulnerability.

"My pleasure," he told her, though his tone didn't echo the sentiment, "but it might be best if we wait until we're married. You need to regain some strength."

Was this some form of sensual harassment, Susan wondered? Did he hope to make her want him so badly that she'd forget everything else? If so, she had to admit that his efforts were successful. She was aching.

Luke was aching too, but he was determined to fight the physical need. Kissing and caressing Susan this morning had temporarily thrown him off balance. Her passionate response had created a deep sensual hunger that threatened his control. Caressing her just now had been an exercise in restraint, but a painfully arousing one.

It had also proven what he'd always suspected. She was a deeply sensual woman who loved the feel of a man's hands on her body. Her soft moans had been genuine. The sight of her nipples pressing against the fabric of her suit was more evidence of her lush sensuality. His muscles clenched at the thought, and he was suddenly impatient to have things settled between them.

"Granddad's seventy-fifth birthday party is a week from today. I'd like to be married by then. That way we can announce it to the family and friends all at once. Get it over with and get on with our lives."

Susan was trying to get her wayward emotions under control. It was difficult to concentrate on what he was saying even though she knew it was incredibly important.

"Couldn't we just announce our engagement next Saturday?"

His eyes flared. "You still have doubts?"

"No." Her reply was truthful. Everything was just happening so fast

Enjoy An Excerpt From

AFTER SUNDOWN: REDEMPTION

“A bodyguard? No—Way!” Alyssa bolted off her seat, and almost stormed right back out the door. “Mr. Maksimovitch, when my publicist set up this appointment it was to acquire some additional personal security, not provide me with a babysitter. I know how to make safe choices. I don’t need anybody to tell me how to do that.”

“I disagree.”

Alyssa swung around at the sound of the unfamiliar male voice behind her. The man was leaning negligently against the doorframe leading into the office. His arms were folded casually across his chest and he appeared very relaxed. His eyes challenged her and he wore a mocking smile on his face. For some reason that smirk irritated her.

“Excuse me? Who are you?” She lifted an eyebrow arrogantly.

“Miss Edwards, this is Christian Galiano,” Vlad explained. He rose from his chair and gave Christian a warning look. “He’s the specialist that I assigned to guar-uh, work with you.”

Christian pushed away from the doorway and strode towards her. His mocking expression suddenly changed to intense interest. Alyssa felt something new replace the irritation she had felt only moments before. Everything became slow motion as the man drew closer. His body moved in a way that seemed unnaturally graceful, as if he were almost gliding towards her rather than walking. Her eyes rose to his, and she couldn’t drag them away. His gaze drew her in, endlessly tugging at her. She felt herself falling into their cognac colored depths.

“Christian!” Vlad yelled.

Christian maintained eye contact with Alyssa until he stood close enough to touch her. He slowly raised his hand to her face. Caught up in his captivating gaze, she had no will to stop him.

"Cristobal! No!"

This time, Christian heeded Vlad's words. He broke eye contact and Alyssa stumbled backwards. She would have fallen against the desk if he hadn't reached out at a speed so fast it blurred to grab her arm and steady her. What had just happened? She felt as if she had been in some sort of daze.

Realizing Christian still held on to her, Alyssa's irritation returned. She tried to pull free, but he didn't release her. Instead, he slowly slid his hand down her arm, over her elbow, skimming his fingers on her wrists before gently enveloping her hand in his.

"It's a pleasure to meet you," he said.

His lilting Spanish accent and light touch left her momentary nonplussed, but she quickly shook it off.

"Nice to meet you, Mr. Galiano. Now if you'd let go of me?"

She looked pointedly down at their clasped hands, then back at him.

"Of course, but please call me Christian," he said, releasing her.

Alyssa stepped back, putting some space between them before turning back towards Mr. Maksimovitch.

"I appreciate your efforts to protect me, however, a bodyguard is not exactly what I had planned," she reiterated.

"You need to change your plan, Ms. Edwards," Christian responded.

"I don't think so," she countered. The man was *really* starting to get on her nerves. "I don't need a man following me around wherever I go, telling me where to go, what to do, or how to do it."

Christian looked like he was about to argue, when Vlad interrupted.

"Miss Edwards. Our business is security. We understand your reluctance to a bodyguard, however, it sounds to me like your problem has become more than just a case of an avid fan wanting your attention. Last night you were attacked. Your physical well being threatened. You managed to escape, but next time you might not be so lucky."

Darn it, the man was right. If he hadn't just voiced her own concerns, she would have been able to refuse their services. Whoever attacked her last night wasn't playing around. She only had two more days until her next speaking appearance. Pride had no place in this. Her life might be at stake.

The two men waited silently for her to make her decision. Christian's expression mocked her, Vlad's looked earnest, concerned. She knew what she had to do.

"Fine," she agreed through gritted teeth. She really didn't like this. "*But,* no offense Mr. Galiano, I'd prefer that you handle my case, Vlad."

Christian's smile remained firmly in place, but Alyssa noticed it now looked like little more than a barring of teeth. Well, that was just too bad. She felt comfortable with Vlad, and definitely uncomfortable with Christian. Something about him screamed a silent warning that said, "stay far away".

"Regretfully, Miss Edwards, that's not possible," Vlad explained. "I'm working on a high profile case of my own at the moment, and won't be able to handle yours as well. Also, please understand that I choose the specialists to work each case based on the specifics of the circumstances. After looking over your situation, and talking to your publicist, I knew that Christian was the one to best handle your needs. I promise you, you'll be satisfied with him and his protection."

Vlad looked pointedly at Christian.

"Isn't that right, Christian?"

Christian looked like the cat that swallowed the cream. His smile widened to wolfish proportions as he met Alyssa's gaze.

"I can definitely satisfy your needs, Miss Edwards. As long as you do as you're told."

Alyssa fumed. The man was just too much! Placing her hands on her hips she met his gaze squarely.

"I don't take orders very well, Mr. Galiano. *And,*" she paused to rake her gaze scathingly over him from head to toe, "my satisfaction is not so easily fulfilled."

When her eyes returned to his face, she could tell by his clenching jaw that he was not amused. Their gazes met and clashed.

"We'll see," he said, before turning to look at Vlad. "I'll leave the details to you, as usual. Just fill me in later."

Christian turned and left the room without a backwards glance.

"Yes, we will," Alyssa, hissed under her breath.

She turned to Vlad with a smile that was most definitely forced.

"I'm sorry, Ms. Edwards. Christian is usually not like this. I promise you, he'll handle your case with the utmost professionalism and courtesy. He is very good at his job. You'll feel safe in his hands," Vlad guaranteed.

"Thank you. I appreciate your confidence in your employees. As you mentioned before, this situation has gotten way out of hand. Everything I've tried up until now hasn't helped."

"Let's go over the events one more time. Tell me everything, from the first time the stalker appeared until now," Vlad requested.

"Of course. It all started after my first motivational talk since being back in Arizona. As you know, I've been traveling around the country promoting my new life therapy book, *Balance*. I scheduled six appearances around the state. I thought it was fitting to finish out my ten-week tour in my home state. Anyway, I was at the Grady Gammage Auditorium in Tempe, when the stalker first contacted me. Everything was going as usual when…"

Why an electronic book?

We live in the Information Age—an exciting time in the history of human civilization, in which technology rules supreme and continues to progress in leaps and bounds every minute of every day. For a multitude of reasons, more and more avid literary fans are opting to purchase e-books instead of paper books. The question from those not yet initiated into the world of electronic reading is simply: *Why?*

1. ***Price.*** An electronic title at Ellora's Cave Publishing and Cerridwen Press runs anywhere from 40% to 75% less than the cover price of the exact same title in paperback format. Why? Basic mathematics and cost. It is less expensive to publish an e-book (no paper and printing, no warehousing and shipping) than it is to publish a paperback, so the savings are passed along to the consumer.
2. ***Space.*** Running out of room in your house for your books? That is one worry you will never have with electronic books. For a low one-time cost, you can purchase a handheld device specifically designed for e-reading. Many e-readers have large, convenient screens for viewing. Better yet, hundreds of titles can be stored within your new library—on a single microchip. There are a variety of e-readers from different manufacturers. You can also read e-books on your PC or laptop computer. (Please note that Ellora's

Cave does not endorse any specific brands. You can check our websites at www.ellorascave.com or www.cerridwenpress.com for information we make available to new consumers.)

3. ***Mobility***. Because your new e-library consists of only a microchip within a small, easily transportable e-reader, your entire cache of books can be taken with you wherever you go.
4. ***Personal Viewing Preferences.*** Are the words you are currently reading too small? Too large? Too... ANNOYING? Paperback books cannot be modified according to personal preferences, but e-books can.
5. ***Instant Gratification.*** Is it the middle of the night and all the bookstores near you are closed? Are you tired of waiting days, sometimes weeks, for bookstores to ship the novels you bought? Ellora's Cave Publishing sells instantaneous downloads twenty-four hours a day, seven days a week, every day of the year. Our webstore is never closed. Our e-book delivery system is 100% automated, meaning your order is filled as soon as you pay for it.

Those are a few of the top reasons why electronic books are replacing paperbacks for many avid readers.

As always, Ellora's Cave and Cerridwen Press welcome your questions and comments. We invite you to email us at Comments@ellorascave.com or write to us directly at Ellora's Cave Publishing Inc., 1056 Home Avenue, Akron, OH 44310-3502.

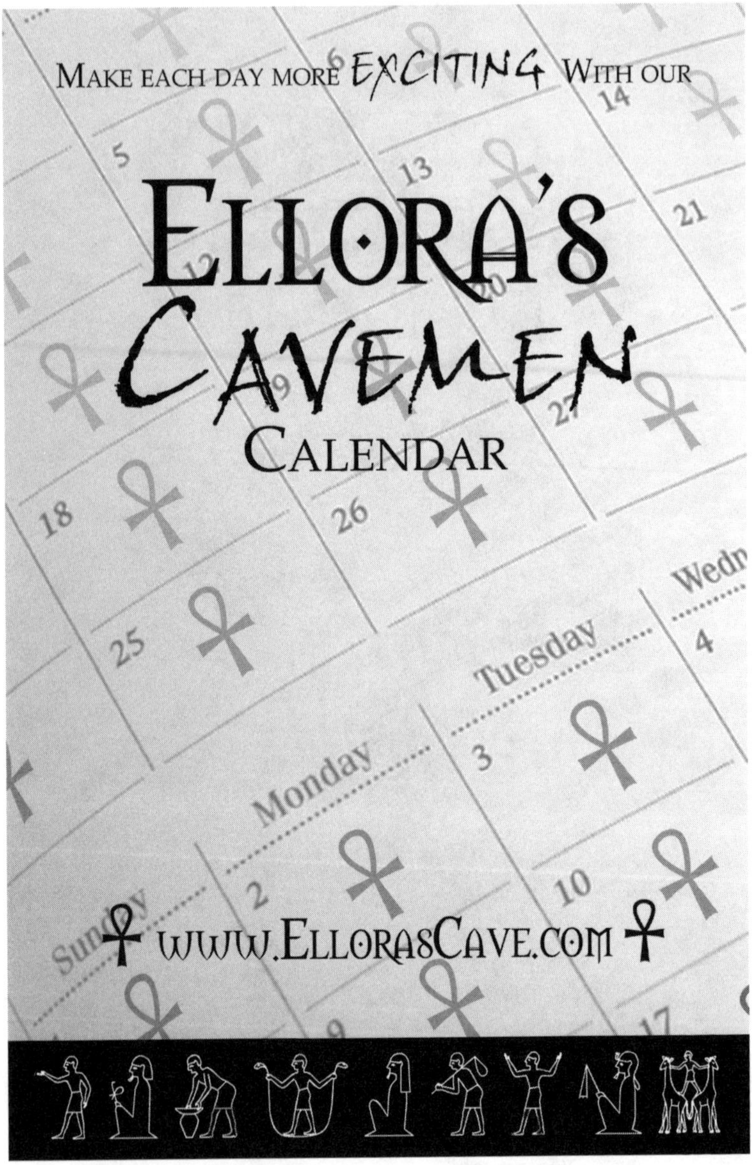
Make each day more EXCITING with our
Ellora's
Cavemen
Calendar
www.EllorasCave.com

Cerridwen Press

Cerridwen, the Celtic goddess of wisdom, was the muse who brought inspiration to storytellers and those in the creative arts.

Cerridwen Press encompasses the best and most innovative stories in all genres of today's fiction.

Visit our website and discover the newest titles by talented authors who still get inspired—much like the ancient storytellers did...

once upon a time.